DOWNLANDERS

A novel by
Frank Haberle

Flexible Press
Minneapolis, Minnesota, 2023

Print ISBN: 979-8-9887213-0-7
eBook ISBN: 979-8-9887213-1-4

Flexible Press LLC
Editors William E Burleson
Vicki Adang, Mark My Words Editorial Services, LLC
Cover William E Burleson

To my sister Mary Patricia Haberle,
1947–1985,
who led the way.

Key characters

Soldiers (Winter 1942):
- Rodney is a court-martialed soldier in a penal unit, sent north.
- Crunch is Rodney's friend, a strongman.

Downlanders (Spring 1983):
- Danny is a hapless clerk, lost and alone in the city.
- Gretch is a travelling surveyor, who Danny meets on a fire escape.
- Buddy is a drug dealer and MBA candidate.
- Fiona, formerly homeless, is Buddy's current girlfriend.
- Freddie is Fiona's brother, deceased, a rescue worker in Grizzle.
- Chief is a pill-addicted petty criminal.
- Droop is another petty criminal.
- Nat is an antique and art collector, formerly an artist.
- Ernie is a former drug addict and current alcoholic, an ex-friend of Buddy.
- Eva, ex-girlfriend of Buddy, is a desert dweller and New Age mystic.

- Bucket-Hat is a clerk at the Fish and Game training center.
- Captain runs the training center.
- Bear Man is a wilderness hippie who talks to bears.
- Rosemarie picks Ernie up hitchhiking.
- Corinne is her copilot.
- Eugene is a traveler Ernie meets at a campsite.
- Barbara is Eugene's wife.
- David is Eva's spiritual advisor.
- Hawk is Chief's old friend, a trail guide.
- Tin Pan Tim is a wanderer Hawk and Chief meet on a trail.
- Sara is a camper Chief meets on a trail.
- Jack is Sara's son.
- Wolf is a Grizzle resident.
- Scout is a backcountry trapper.

"He who jumps into the void owes no explanation
to those who stand and watch."
—Jean-Luc Goddard

DOWNLANDERS

JANUARY 1942

Rodney shakes the cold
from his bones

Rodney pulls his duffel bag up and onto his shoulder, and he takes his place in line behind two hundred other 65ers. They fall into step like they were trained to do. Together they ascend a long ramp from the storage tank of the rusting freighter and march out onto a strange, frozen dock. And they stand there and shiver and wait. And then they stand there and shiver and wait some more.

For ten days, they had huddled in the damp darkness of a ship's hold, squatting in sawdust, listening to large, alien waves lapping against the hull, or waiting for the hissing of a torpedo that never came. It was hot and damp in the hold, poorly lit by bare bulbs that dangled from the girders above them. On the deck, they could hear other soldiers stomping or laughing or fighting; but they never made contact with the other soldiers. The little round windows were painted black from the outside, so they had little idea where they were headed.

Now, stepping out into the night, the 65ers drink deep drafts of cold air and look out onto an alien landscape. On a long pier, they sit on their duffel bags, huddled together in summer fatigues with thin blankets draped over their shoulders. They wait out an unthinkably cold, wet wind, blowing down from what looks like a huge blue tub of ice climbing into the sky just across the sound and spilling straight out into the bay across from them.

After some hours, shadows sink into the bay. Rodney watches a converted ocean liner, painted dark gray, tie up to the next pier. Within minutes, a large deployment of sandy-haired infantry troops, all with buckled green parkas and fur-lined caps, unloads onto the dock. Those soldiers put down their gear by a line of trucks and stroll into a row of bars and restaurants facing the docks.

"Say, sergeant," the 65ers' unofficial leader, a huge man they call Crunch, calls to one of the military police standing in front of them holding his baton with two hands, "can we go get something to eat?"

"What's wrong?" the sergeant asks, eying the "P" sewn into Crunch's shoulder, just above the "5" patch. "Wasn't the prison cuisine good enough for you?"

"I'd just like to go get something to eat, sir."

The MP's fists clench more tightly around the baton. "You stay right where you are," he says. "Those are the orders."

"Sergeant, where are we?"

"At the war. Where do you think you are?"

"I thought the war was over."

"Yeah, me too. We all thought the war was over."

"If we're at the war, then where's the fighting?"

The MP stares up toward the mountain ledges and grunts.

"Your guess is as good as mine."

Sitting huddled against the wind, Rodney can do nothing but shiver and worry. He's never done cold before; he's never experienced the sensation. He tries to keep still. Doubts quickly and persistently sink into his mind whenever he is still, which has happened often in the last few months. The 65ers sat still for days on a stifling, suffocating train crossing. They sat for two weeks in sheds on the piers by this strange new ocean, watching huge armadas of soldiers and gear load up and pack out for somewhere else. Finally, their turn came; they climbed together into the cavernous belly of what was clearly the last available floating boat.

Rodney's military life had become marathons of stillness, punctuated by random and brutal tests of endurance and by cruelly indifferent screams of an endless rotation of ranking strangers. There is little difference between the military and the military prison he found himself in for no explained reason. Each forced march, each round of calisthenics delivered to them in the prison camp, on train platforms, on docks, and in the dark hold of the cold floating vessel, all take him farther from the sweet, hot, familiar monotony of what he remembers as home.

The image that keeps worrying Rodney is the face of his little brother, Perce, thirteen years old, turning away from him at the train station they debarked from. Although it is now months and thousands of miles behind him, Rodney's mind has built a trap around Perce's face, framed with the wild, dizzy, shattered look of the newly lost. Perce had tried to keep his head up above a crowd that pushed and shoved him around a train platform. Rodney yelled to him through his train window, to wave him off in the direction they had walked into the little city, but Perce could not see him. Rodney knew he himself was lost in the dinging and clanging of the train's coupled cars shifting into motion, the scream of the chugging engine, the smoke and steam spilling into the windows, and the pained shifting of the young men in the train, packed together, screaming and waving and lurching over each other for a last glance of a loved one through the sealed train windows. Perce was buried between perfumed mothers and after-shaved dads all holding handkerchiefs, screaming and waving back at the train. "That way!" Rodney yelled to Perce, waving. He caught one last glance of Perce's rectangular head, the short-cropped hair and hatless head bobbing above the surface, turning around, seeking a direction, and then disappearing into the large, shimmering mass, as the train, Rodney's train, containing the 65th and various other regiments, broke from the luminous cavern of the station and wrapped itself into the dark, tangled tracks of the countryside. He'll make it home all right, Rodney told himself, squeezing back into his rock-hard bench between two uniformed strangers who smelled like soup. He'll figure it out, Rodney thought.

The farther from home he got, the less able Rodney was to shake the image from his head. He worried ceaselessly about his brother, then his mother; where the money would come from, how they would eat, the hostile neighbors all around them. Rodney wrote static, fast postcards at every mail stop, asking his mother to update him on how things were. In the hold of the freighter, he'd written three more, but in this strange new place, Rodney had no idea where he was or how he could send the notes. They were still in his pocket.

Now Rodney scans the muddy road separating the town from the docks, searching for a post office or mailbox, but he knows he can't leave his spot. Darkness starts brushing against the docks. The beams of headlights flash as another row of uncovered flatbed trucks crawl slowly toward them. The trucks park at the end of the dock.

"Here you go, boys," the MP yells, blowing his whistle. "That there's your golden chariot." The soldiers rise and stretch their stiff legs, trying to shake the cold from their bones.

They pile onto the flatbeds and pack in closely, thirty or forty men on each, legs dangling off the sides or crossed up under their chins.

"How long a ride is it?" Clutch, next to Rodney, yells at one of the drivers, who is lighting a cigarette for the MP.

"Not so far," the driver says.

"Well, that's certainly a relief," Clutch says to Rodney, closing his eyes and pulling his legs up more tightly. "At least we'll have some hot chow soon."

The ride lasts eight hours without a break. The trucks ride up new dirt roads in the dark. Soon everyone is wet and frozen. The men on the perimeter hold on for their lives. Just beyond the trucks' dim yellow headlights is an unimaginable darkness, a forest more deep and tangled than any swamp they'd seen in their hazy, sultry home states. Occasionally a branch sweeps through, banging heads, seemingly sweeping a row of soldiers into the darkness.

At one moment, the convoy rises onto a ridge. Those whose eyes are not yet frozen shut can make out, through the branches, the warm lights of a town in the distance. Their hopes rise until the lights fade behind them.

Lucky to be placed in the center of the truck, his legs folded tightly up under his chin, Rodney tries to move his toes to make sure they are not frozen. To stay warm, he tries to recall the shimmering heat that rises like smoke each morning from the cornfields surrounding the one-room cabin he shares with his mother and Perce, growing right up to the porch. But in an instant, he is worrying again. He remembers the day he left, following his four-day furlough. Limping on swollen legs, his mother saw him to the porch. Rodney expected her to cry, but she just stared out past him into the rows of corn, like she was already looking for him to return.

"Try and eat something, will you, Rodney," she said. "You've gotten so very skinny. You are all bones."

Perce ran down the steps excitedly. He'd grown six inches since Rodney got his draft notice, but he was clumsy, all elbows and knees. He picked up Rodney's duffel bag and threw it over his back, almost throwing himself to the ground with it. Hunched over, he turned to their mother. "Can I walk him up a ways, Ma?" he begged. "Up toward town, just a ways?"

"You can walk him up a ways," their mother said. "But don't you dare set foot in that town. That isn't your town, Perce. You tell him, Rodney."

Through the afternoon, Rodney and Perce walked side by side, each holding a strap of the duffel bag. The heat was unbelievable; it blew across browned, flattened fields in a thick haze that yellowed the trees. There was no shade along the road. "By god, I'm thirsty," Perce said.

"I'll buy you a soda when we get to town," Rodney said. "We'll go into town, I'll buy you a soda, and send you on your way."

In the town, they found no place to buy a soda, and they walked all the way into the station. Tired and thirsty—and growingly anxious about where he was headed with the war heating up everywhere—Rodney didn't give it a thought, until the train started pulling away, that his little brother might not know how to get home.

At dawn the trucks finally stop in a clearing. Whistles shriek all around them. Those who can still walk after the long truck ride—and the prior boat ride and the cross-country train in which they were stuffed for two weeks—march through a towering forest. The ground is frozen, crunching under their boots. There is a dusting of snow in the branches—for many, the first they've ever really seen up close. Rodney reaches out and holds snow in his fingers until it burns. If it's cold, he thinks, why does it burn? He shows it to Crunch, who shakes his head.

"We haven't seen the last of that, for sure," Crunch says.

The trail opens onto a dirt road. The remaining 65ers are ordered to line up. A row of crates, half of them broken open and lying on their sides, sit in the thawing mud in the middle of the road. An officer with a walrus moustache and a belly sticking out of an undersized bomber jacket stands up on one of the crates, staring at them with contempt. Then he starts speaking into a bullhorn.

"Boys, I suppose you're wondering what you're doing out here in this godforsaken, crap-shot, frozen hellhole, and not out in some tropical paradise with the rest of the army."

Rodney glimpses quickly down the line. He quickly estimates that at least a quarter of the 65ers are no longer with them; stuck behind them on broken trucks or frozen to death in the wilderness. It's time to stop worrying about Perce, he thinks to himself. Forget Perce. It's time to start worrying about myself.

"Well, I have news for you, boys," the officer continues, wiping his nose. "We have a new enemy, and he is here. He has landed some eight hundred miles in that direction." The officer waves the bullhorn in one direction, then, correcting himself, in another direction. "In that direction. He is just eight hundred miles from here, at the tip of this peninsula that we are on now. An eight hundred–mile peninsula. And it is our job to stop him from getting any farther."

"All right," Crunch hisses through his clenched teeth, standing next to Rodney. All of the men are shivering violently. "I'm finally going to get my hands on a gun."

"It's our job, boys, to build a road," the officer continues. He seems awfully young to be an officer, Rodney thinks. He obviously prepared this speech and is quite pleased with it.

"A road that will meet the enemy head-on," the officer continues. "A road that drives a stake straight through this forest, eight hundred miles, straight down this peninsula and straight down the enemy's throat. A road that will provide a lifeline of munitions and supplies our troops will need to win this war."

"Troops?" Crunch whispers. "Aren't we the troops?"

The officer climbs down, removes his black leather gloves for dramatic effect, takes a crowbar from one of his orderlies, and struggles to crack open one of the crates. "We're in the fight now, boys," the officer says and grunts. But he cannot break the crate open; he curses and heaves with all of his strength.

"'Scuse me for asking, sir," Crunch says, "but I don't quite understand. When are we gonna get our weapons? When are we going to fight the enemy?"

Four soldiers have stepped forward to help the officer, who appears to have not heard anything. They take the crowbar from him, and one of them cracks the case; it springs open. A dozen axes, four huge saws, and another dozen shovels fall out into the snow. Crunch stares at the tools, stooped in disappointment.

Fighting to catch his breath, the officer bends down and picks up an axe. "These are our weapons, boys!" he says for effect, waving the axe weakly in the air. Rodney looks at Crunch. Crunch looks at Rodney. Then the officer points the axe at the dark forest ahead of them—first to his right, and then, correcting himself, to his left. "And this here wild land, this here frozen, dark hell. *This is our enemy!*"

MARCH 1983

FROM *THE ONLY PLANET GUIDE:* WELCOME TO GRIZZLE!

For anyone who has ever stared out the window from their mundane lives and said dreamily, "I want to drop everything, quit, and take off for X," this guidebook bears exciting news! You can now fill in the "X." The Grizzle Peninsula, the mysterious eight hundred–mile land mass jutting like a crumbling question mark into the sea, is officially open for travel. This, the first edition of The Only Planet Guide to Grizzle, *will tell you how to get there, what to bring, what to expect, what not to expect—and most important, how to get home safely—with stories and memories to last you a lifetime.*

After sleeping for thirty years under classified military restrictions, the government partially opened the Grizzle Peninsula in 1975 to limited commercial trade and development with military operations moved to outposts on surrounding islands. In 1982 these restrictions were fully lifted, opening the entire peninsula to recreational use. Since then, summer traffic has accelerated. Several of the region's most spectacular sites—particularly the Great Gulf Wilderness—have been set aside temporarily as regional parks. But many coastal regions are already being consumed by a vast, growing empire of oil refineries or clear-cut by the resurgent timber industry. Unpaved gravel roads connect small, isolated settlements built around military way stations, or settled beforehand, carved out of the wilderness by pioneers who staked their claims long before the army got there. These little settlements survived the thirty-year military occupation and are booming today.

For backpackers, wanderers, searchers who seek wilderness adventure on a low budget, the opening of the Grizzle Peninsula brings good news and bad.

The good news is, for the first time in generations, you will have access to an unspoiled paradise that boggles the imagination. Untouched for years, the Grizzle Peninsula offers a luminous palate of endless old-growth forests, snow-capped volcanic peaks, spectacular rocky shorelines, and an endless parade of wildlife. Challenging driving conditions slow the long line of RV campers and recreational tourists to a trickle, preserving much of the off-road pristine wilderness for those willing to get their feet wet. Beyond the rough road there are legends of a bohemian subset who slipped into the wilds during the occupation to create self-sustaining settlements, most notably the rumored little village of Grizzletown, somewhere at the farthest reaches of the peninsula.

But there is also potentially bad news for the wilderness crowd. As of this writing, the government has big plans for selling the entire peninsula to private interests: the eastern coastline to big oil, the interior to timber companies, and a four-lane highway connecting the Petrolia airport with ski resort developments in the Great Gulf region.

The bottom line is this: If you've ever dreamed of going to a place like the Grizzle Peninsula, you'd better get there quick. And if you do choose to go, this first (and hopefully not last) edition of The Only Planet Guide to Grizzle—the go-to source for information on tramping, beatnicking, and backpacking the Grizzle Peninsula—will tell you how to get to our planet's last, greatest, and briefly unspoiled wilderness. Beyond explaining the history and geography of this great wilderness, this guide will tell you:

- *How to get there and how to get around, including different ways to travel to and across the peninsula on a budget (this guide is geared for car and non-car travelers).*

- *Where to stay, with detailed descriptions of the municipal and wilderness campgrounds along the way, as well as boardinghouses, inns geared for budget travelers (with pricing for each), "secret campsites," and back country camping where backpackers can stay for free.*

- *What to do, with each regional description (for the Portia Region, Great Gulf Wilderness, Petrolia Region, and Outer Grizzle) broken down by activities so you'll know the best places to day hike, back-pack, fish, kayak, eat, drink, explore, and be merry.*

- *How to stay safe, with the guidance of an experienced back-country traveler and explorer who will provide insight in how to survive: what to bring, what to expect, and how to get help when you need it.*

Danny stands alone
on a fire escape

Danny stands alone on a steel fire escape, staring in through the window at a party. Inside, three dozen strangers are swaying back and forth to a Debbie Reynolds show tune. They surround a bald giant in a yellow radiation suit. Sweat dripping off his nose, laughing maniacally, the giant pours kamikazes from a large green pitcher into plastic cups held out all around him.

Danny climbed out onto the fire escape with somebody he knew from work, who went back in for a beer and never came back. Now he's alone in the damp air, trying to gather the courage to climb back in through the window and push his way to the door and the street.

A woman climbs out onto the fire escape and stands next to him. "I just couldn't stand it in there," she says. "All that cigarette smoke. Do you smoke?"

"No, I quit," Danny says.

"'Cause if you do, hey, it's okay, I don't mind. It's not my party. But where I come from, people don't smoke like that."

"I quit," Danny says. "I don't smoke."

"Hey, you do what you like. Wow! You're a big one, aren't you? You want a beer? I got two here." In the darkness, she is little more than a silhouette. Her name is Gretch. She's visiting from someplace far away. It's her last night in the city. Tomorrow she's traveling to Grizzle, she says, to do some surveying work.

"Grizzle. Wow. I'm dying to go to Grizzle," Danny says.

"Oh, yeah? You a backpacker or something?"

"Oh, yeah," Danny says. For a good five minutes, he listens to himself speak with great expertise on the subject of backpacking, although he has not done much of it and not in many years. He finishes with an embellished survival story, equal parts heroic and self-effacing, that makes her laugh.

"Well, you should definitely go to Grizzle while you can," she says. Her eyes capture a glint of a headlight passing below. "I go up there every summer."

"Every summer?" Danny asks.

"Oh, sure," she says. "I went up five years ago to find work, and I just got hooked on the place. Now I got work up there. I get paid to go into the backcountry. Mountains, bears, volcanoes. You name it."

"Wow," Danny says. The thought of actually doing something like this, of breaking away from this deadening city and this deadening job and venturing into real, distant wilderness, suddenly grips him. "Was it hard to get work up there?"

"Well," she says, "it wasn't so hard that first year. And now you can always get a job with the parks or in a fish factory or something. When I first went up there, I wasn't a surveyor yet. I worked on a fishing boat."

"A fishing boat," Danny says, gulping his beer dreamily.

"Yeah. It was five summers ago. Let me see—was it five? I was done with all this, and I just started hitchhiking. Nothing bad ever happened. I remember getting dumped by a logging truck where the Soldier's Highway peels off into the woods. I was stuck there eight hours. It was raining. I carved something in a signpost—what was it? 'If miles were smiles, my teeth would be hurting.' If you go up there, you should check it out. I'm sure it's still there on that signpost, right at the end of the exit ramp.

"So then I made it all the way out to Can-Town without a hassle, and I set up my tent on a beach. I walked up and down the docks that day, asked every boat if they needed a worker.

They all laughed at me, said stupid things, because I'm a girl, I guess, or because I'm small. But I asked every one of them.

"That night I went back to my tent, and there was a tent pitched next to it. A young guy named Roy, sitting in front of a fire, seventeen, maybe eighteen. He just hitched in too. He was scareder than hell. I took him for a beer, to a bar there, the Salty Dawg. You'd love it. You should check it out. So I'm sitting there with Roy, skinny little kid, ran away from home. We're elbow up in the bar, and it's the first bar he's ever been in in his whole life, and there's a fight every ten minutes, and he's shaking like a leaf.

"Then this guy stares over at me. Then he gets up and sits next to me. He says, 'You're the lady who was looking for work today. You ever worked big fish?' I tell him the truth. I say, 'No.' 'Well, look,' he said, and I looked at him, and he was, you know, a normal-looking guy, not too psycho or anything. 'My crew walked out on me today, and I'm sailing tomorrow. You and your friend want to work, get out there at 6 a.m., third pier, *Lucky Lady,* blue boat. But you're gonna work, believe me.' And that was that, and there we were."

Screams come from inside the apartment. The man in the radiation suit has fallen down. Through the window, Danny can see the man's face turning purple, panicked. Someone is trying to unplug the air hose in the back of the helmet.

"Thing with big fish," Gretch continues, leaning over the fire escape railing and staring down at the garbage cans three flights below, "is that you hit them or you don't. Couple of dozen boats sailed out of Can-Town that morning in every direction. I was supposed to cook and chop bait; Roy was supposed to bait hooks. You let chains down on winches with maybe a hundred hooks in them. Roy couldn't hack it, and then he got sick.

"We were rocking on waves so high you couldn't see over them. I was chopping, baiting, and taking care of Roy, who was throwing up and crying for his mommy. Guy who owned the boat kept yelling down to me from the bridge, 'Just keep them going!' This went on for eighteen hours. Then we trawled and rested. At dawn we started hauling them in. I never seen such a thing. Hook them and drag them on board, and these are the big fish too! That was the sick part. Batting them in the head with a baseball bat, kicking them into the hold, slipping on the blood and the scales. The fish just stare up at you, wide-eyed. They want to know why you're doing this to them. It was sick. It was sick.

"When we got done, we did it all over again, and then we sailed home. Every muscle in my body was pulled, my hands were laced with cuts, and my clothes were all soaked in fish juice. But at the end of three days, he handed me $1,800 in cash. Roy got that much too. I don't know why. But that was plenty enough to get Roy home and me on the boat out to the islands, where I got a job in a fish factory. Five bucks an hour. Sixteen hours a day. Forty-six straight days. That's where I met my prince charming, Billy. Boy, did he screw me over."

Danny can just make out the silhouette of her shoulders as she shrugs and drains her beer can. "Yep," she says, softly smiling, bathed in just a brush of gray light. "I made pretty good money that summer."

She looks Danny up and down. "You should definitely check out Grizzle. You want to come next time? I'm a free-lancer, so nobody cares. I'm always looking for a helper. I need somebody to watch my back for bears while I survey. You don't have to carry my stuff or nothing. Here's my card." She puts a little piece of paper in his hand. "Drop me a line if you want."

Suddenly, the beers' warming confidence drains out of Danny. "Um, thanks, maybe I will," he stammers. "I gotta go meet somebody."

"I can't pay you or nothing, but it'll be worth it, believe me. Think it over is all I'm saying." She laughs, watching Danny climb through the window. "Well, nice to meet you!"

Sitting alone at the end of a bar fifteen minutes later, Danny looks over the card. *Gretchen Maloney*, it reads. *Industrial Surveyor*. "Grizzle," Danny mutters to himself when his beer arrives. "Like I'm ever going to get up and go to Grizzle."

Fiona weighs
her options

At the other end of the bar, Fiona Gallagher sits on a barstool next to her boyfriend, Buddy Jones. The bar is long and narrow and filled with smoke. Earlier, during the day, old men came to the bar to warm up and get drunk and smoke in silence and peace while their livers and spleens shriveled within them. After the sun set, the old men had hobbled home. Now the bar is filled with bright-eyed graduate students, glowing about their futures. A big lopey guy sits at the far end alone, out of place, staring into his beer, lost in thought.

Buddy sells pharmaceutical drugs to support his more refined drug needs and, on occasion, to pay for business school. Right now he buys beers, and then shots, which he throws down at a pretty steady clip. He buys them with Fiona's last $200 from her most recent temp job. He hit a slow patch recently with the pharmaceutical business, and his own stash is running low; he's worried about money for the first time in a long time. He stares up at a baseball game on a TV mounted in the corner, but he can't tell who's playing or what the score is.

Next to Buddy, Fiona stares at the long line of bottles behind the bar. The labels whisper of exotic places. A camel saunters in front of the pyramids. Seals bark from the edge of icebergs. A Mountie salutes from a horse, surrounded by snowy mountains.

"I really want to visit my brother next summer," Fiona says.

"Your brother? Mister Grizzle?" Buddy snorts. "Mister helicopter rescue man?"

Buddy's squinting eyes have wandered down the bar toward two college girls talking to a man in a suit, who's way too young to be wearing a suit. Fiona looks down the bar for the big lopey guy who was sitting alone, hoping he met somebody or joined the mingling crowds, but he is gone; his empty mug sits sadly on the bar. Then she turns to look at Buddy, who recently has started to look way too old for twenty-five—pale and patchy and jowly—and has lost all the edges she was drawn to three years ago. *I settle for things way too easily,* she thinks.

"I just think it's time for a little break," she says. "A real trip. You can come too. If you want."

"Yeah, well. When I met you, you were living on a bench in the park," Buddy says. "Now *that* must have been a real trip."

Fiona doesn't say anything.

"I'm not going way out to Grizzle," Buddy says. "I wouldn't get caught dead out there. You know who goes out there? The losers who flunk out here. They think they're finding themselves out there. They're not finding anything out there. They either come back with their tails tucked between their legs, or they fall off the ledges into the sea. Your brother excluded, of course." Buddy throws down a shot and bangs the glass on the table. "I mean, I guess he gets to fly around in helicopters and help find the losers' bodies floating around or something. But no, thanks for me. I'm getting an internship next summer. I got better things to do than to go out there."

Buddy continues staring at the girls. Fiona continues searching the labels of the bottles. She thinks of her brother Freddie and the photo he sent with his helmet and sunglasses on, smiling, standing in front of a helicopter. Beyond the helicopter, there's a chain-link fence; beyond that, dark pine forest winding up to a snowy, twisted peak. Clouds swirl in a blue-green haze; it's hard to see where the mountain ends and the sky begins.

"I just mean, go out there for a visit," she says. "I didn't mean we should go out and try to live up there."

"Nobody lives there," Buddy says. "People just die there."

Later, Buddy and Fiona stumble up the stairs to their fourth-floor walk-up, the apartment that Fiona barely makes rent for each month while Buddy goes to school. Like the bar, the street, and the staircase, the apartment is long and narrow. Buddy turns on the single fluorescent light. On a crate by the couch is a phone and an answering machine. The message light blinks red three times, then pauses, then blinks three more times. Buddy swerves toward the table and pushes a button on his way to the kitchen. Fiona sits down on the couch, the same place she always sits. "You have six messages," the machine says and then beeps. Buddy pulls open the kitchen door and takes out two cans of Miller. The first five messages are predictable. "Hey, Buddy, where are you, man?" The sixth is a garbled voice she doesn't recognize, mumbling into the tape recorder. "Need to call immediately," it says, then muffles before a next beep, then another. Then the machine goes silent.

"Who was that?" Fiona asks.

"I dunno," Buddy says. He's pulled his gear out of a drawer. "You first?"

"No, you go," Fiona says. "Can you play it again?"

"Don't be a drama queen." Buddy shrugs and starts rolling up his sleeve.

"Can you please just play it again?"

But Buddy isn't listening. While she ties the cord, he picks up the channel changer and flicks on the screen. "Check it out, cool," he says. "The new Dire Straits video."

Fiona does what she does. It's like taking care of a cow, she thinks to herself. All the tying off and pumping and milking. Now I'm becoming a cow too, she thinks. Do I really want to become a cow?

Buddy nods into the other world; his eyes are open, but they are gone. Soon Fiona starts drifting too. Her eyes drift around the room. The couch lifts gently. The TV drifts away. The light from the answering machine still blinks, somewhere near the corner of Fiona's eye. Buddy stares hard into the screen, then falls asleep sitting upright on the couch. Fiona's eyes drift around the room until they settle on the photo of her little brother, Freddie, beaming at her from the refrigerator door. She thinks of the envelope Freddie sent her with the application and the paperwork. I have to tell Buddy, Fiona thinks. He starts snoring next to her, his head fallen back, his mouth wide open. Fiona turns back to the answering machine. She thinks of Freddie, her little brother. Then she looks at the answering machine. And suddenly she knows that something has gone terribly, terribly wrong.

Eva meets Ernie
at the airport

Fortified by his five-beer flight, Ernie O'Connell's legs carry him perfectly, deliberately up the ramp from the airplane to the airport terminal. Ernie is all but certain that he's here to spend three days hiking in a canyon desert with Eva, his long-lost roommate Buddy's long-forgotten ex. At the thought of Buddy, who he hasn't seen in a couple of years, Ernie winces. Ernie's pretty sure that Eva called him out of the blue a month ago, and they had a really good and friendly conversation, the first time they'd spoken in a few years. But now he realizes that this may have never happened. After replacing his unsteady drug addiction with a steady, more reliable alcohol addiction, Ernie's brain still ventures freely between his own truths and myths. As he looks out at the sea of strange faces at the end of the ramp, Ernie accepts that he probably made this whole thing up about Eva, and he took this flight out to the desert for nothing.

Then he sees Eva, waving. She sparkles like she always did, but she's changed. She's tan and relaxed. She stands differently, more comfortably. She's in cutoff shorts and hiking boots, an untucked floral shirt, a blue-beaded leather necklace, and red-beaded earrings. She startles Ernie. She gives him a strong, assertive hug. She smells like cocoa.

"I can't believe it!" she says. "You finally came out here!"

They step outside the terminal. The air is hot, clean, and dry. Ernie follows Eva to an older model Datsun station wagon with a cracked windshield. Ernie puts his backpack, filled with camping gear and boots he pulled from the box in his closet, into the back of the car. After several efforts, he gets the trunk to latch. Eva drives through a labyrinth of curving streets between one-story cottages with red roofs and little rock gardens. Ernie speaks in short bursts about the flight, the airplane food, the cab ride, how cool each little rock garden is. Eva listens, laughs, agrees, and says "wow" repeatedly.

Her cottage is tiny, set back behind twisted brush on a hillside. In the kitchen, there's a table with two mismatched chairs. In a small frame on a shelf, there's a picture of Eva with another woman and two long-haired, tanned young men, all in parkas, standing in a snowfield at some unthinkable altitude. An ornate native wall hanging covers the wall. She offers Ernie a beer. There are two in the refrigerator. Ernie drinks both; she has herbal tea. They pack their backpacks and list everything they'll need for the hike: She has a stove, fuel, food, water bottles, filter, and tent—although she usually sleeps with her head outside the tent in the desert, she points out.

"What about, you know, snakes?" Ernie says.

"They're more likely to climb into your sleeping bag with you for heat than to bite you," she says. "Thing is not to get them upset."

"Oh. Scorpions?"

"It's best to avoid them."

They go out to dinner. Ernie drinks another four beers. He brings up Buddy, just to connect the dots; while he hadn't spoken to him in a long time, Ernie had heard that Buddy was trying to get through business school. Eva listens patiently; she hasn't heard from Buddy since they broke up. Neither one mentions the drugs.

"Buddy," she says, smiling and shaking her head.

"Yeah, Buddy," Ernie says, shaking his.

There's a dance somewhere in the restaurant. There are swirling bright lights and people laughing and live music and applause spilling in from another room. Ernie starts telling stories about his city life. The tales seem to fit together seamlessly. Ernie moves from the complicated balancing act he feels he performs at his clerical job, to the remarkable, sensitive way he manages tensions and altercations on the streets and the buses, to his unflinching perception of the aesthetics and symmetry of the post-industrial landscape. As the evening goes on, Ernie's stories become more elaborate. They seem reasonable and funny and honest and interesting as he says them, less so as they sit on the table between Ernie and Eva.

Eva speaks very little. She follows Ernie's stories, laughing when Ernie hopes she'll laugh, opening her eyes wide at other parts. She says "wow" at least thirty times.

"Anyhow," Ernie says, "it's all been closing in on me recently, in so many ways. I really think I need to start changing some things."

The waitress brings the check, and Ernie realizes he's been doing all of the talking.

"Anyhow," Ernie says, "I've been doing all the talking."

Eva looks down at the label of the beer bottle she's been peeling all night. She understands needing to change things. Sometimes people close in on her too. Her friends are great; they're teaching her so many things, about herself, her powers and energies. But it's hard. Ernie asks her what she means, and she shrugs. Someday, she says. Someday I'll try to explain it.

They drive back to her house. She turns in; they need to get an early start. Ernie rolls his sleeping bag out on her couch and stares at the ceiling. The air in the apartment is cool, mountain air, desert air.

Ernie remembers the restaurant. He talked too much. His body flinches impulsively. What was he talking about? Why does he talk so much?

Then Ernie looks across the room in the dim light at the photograph. Who are these other people? Boyfriends? Road dudes? Ernie used to think he was a road dude. Before he met Eva, he'd hitchhiked, worked odd jobs, and backpacked everywhere. Every day he daydreams about being a road dude again. As the seasons pass, the daydreams stay. But in real life, Ernie became another guy at a desk, on the bus, on a barstool. Ernie became another guy going home alone with a six-pack and a takeout burrito.

The couch rises and swirls, gently tonight, not spinning wildly like the prior night. Ernie's first dream floats back into the restaurant to the music. Ernie's the road dude in the picture; he's been together with Eva all this time. Ernie's holding Eva in his arms and dancing, slowly, the lights spinning away from him. Everything smells like cocoa.

Suddenly Ernie's awake; it's the first hint of daylight. Eva's made a pot of coffee for Ernie and a cup of tea for herself. She pours Ernie's coffee into a thermos while he rolls up his sleeping bag. In seconds, they're back in the car and driving up a highway. The city peels away, and they're in the suburbs, then the desert. Ernie stares out the cracked windshield at a landscape that is totally new to him—wild desert with huge cactus and tumbleweeds, red cracked mountain ranges shimmering on the horizon.

After a few hours, Eva turns into a one-lane dirt road. She pulls over under a cluster of twisted pine trees. She climbs out, sits on the back of the car, and ties on her hiking boots. Ernie follows her to the back of the car. He pulls his own boots out. Ernie hasn't worn them in many years, but when he laces them up, they feel familiar and sturdy. When he pulls his pack on, he feels ready to go.

"It's really good to get away," she says.

"Yeah," Ernie says. But he remembers his dream, and a wave of embarrassment passes through him. He tries not to look at her.

Eva walks to a ledge where the sky disappears. Ernie follows her to the rim. A thousand shades of red and orange glare up from below.

"All the way down there?" Ernie asks.

"That's the plan."

"Are you sure we brought enough water?"

"There's water down there."

"What about food? What if we get stuck down there?"

"We've got food for an extra day. Come on."

Eva pulls her pack out from the back of the car and deftly swings it up onto her shoulders. She steps over the rim, onto a trail clinging to the canyon's wall. Ernie focuses on her backpack and follows.

Bobbing down the incline in front of him, Eva looks so strong, brown and lean from her years in the desert. She's a different person now. Ernie remembers her years before, in the crowded gridlines of the city, the brief girlfriend of Buddy the dealer. She was so unsure of herself. Out here she's all business.

Ernie nurses a bottle of water. He has two more in his pack. He wraps a bandanna around his head; in seconds it's soaked. Sweat pours off his nose. He wrings out the bandana, then struggles to keep pace with Eva, who moves with steady determination down the trail. Ernie realizes he'll have nothing to drink other than water for the next two nights; he struggles to remember the last time he went through a night without a drink, and it's been years. What if he freaks out? What if he can't take it? Better not to think about it. So he tries not to think about anything.

Hours pass. The sun shifts in the sky. Shadows pour down from the high cliffs into deep black pools. The trail plunges in jagged switchbacks to the floor of the canyon. Ernie looks up to the cliffs now soaring above him, the same cliffs he will eventually have to climb back up. The alcohol has evaporated from his body. Ernie's first clear thought is a new wave of terror, deeper than the rest. What if he can't get back up? What if he dies down here? People die in the desert all the time. What if there is no water?

Ernie stumbles forward, following Eva down into a narrow passage. As if on cue, water cascades from mossy walls, over broken rocks, and under Ernie's feet. He stops to plunge his head in the creek. He refills his water bottles. The panic is still there. And then he looks around at the bubbling moss, the rock formations like cathedral apses, the rock faces like carved saints. Water seeps out everywhere, here at the bottom of a canyon in the desert. He decides that all the tension of his other world, his city world, just can't matter right now. All that matters is that he keeps following Eva, now a silhouette down the sandbar, turning a corner.

A fine line of sunlight brushes against the uppermost rim. The sky fades to deep blue, and the first stars appear. Eva moves in the shadows and disappears around a corner. Suddenly the corridor opens up. A foaming brown river surges toward Ernie. On a beach, he finds Eva sitting by a large ring of stones, detaching her tent.

"Are we the only people down here?" Ernie asks.

"I don't see anybody else. Come on, give me a hand."

The moon rises full over the rim of the canyon, bathing the walls blue. They eat dinner in silence. Ernie stares out at the river. It bubbles like chocolate milk. He's sweated pounds of fluids out of his body, replaced them with gallons of creek water. He feels different now. Somehow, for the moment, he feels clear-headed. He feels good.

After dinner, Eva walks up the beach. She disappears behind a rock. She comes back a minute later, her tangled black hair glittering wet in the dim light. Ernie and Eva arrange their sleeping bags so their heads are outside the tent. Ernie watches the moon inch higher into the sky.

"Do you ever think of just breaking out altogether?" Eva asks.

"Breaking out?"

"Yeah, just taking off? Leaving everything behind? Just the great big nothing up ahead?"

"This isn't the great big nothing?"

"No, I mean really taking off. Like upland, the end of the road, the Grizzle Peninsula, the backcountry. Like, just keep going, as far as you can go. See where it all goes."

Ernie freezes. What should he say? What's the right thing to say?

"I've always wanted to go to Grizzle," Ernie says.

They lay in silence for a long time. Ernie wants to say something more. He tries to form the words. But when the jumble of letters falls into place, when Ernie finally has the courage to say something, Eva's eyes are closed. Her eyes are closed, and she's sleeping, and Ernie's said nothing, and he knows he never will, so long as she's awake; that this will all be over in a few days, and he'll be off, back to the city.

But now she's sleeping, and so it's safe for Ernie to whisper: "Let's go, let's go, let's go."

Chief goes for
a ride

It's one of those plastic push-button telephones on a milk crate in the common space. This morning it rings violently, pulling Robert "Chief" Bocci out of his sweet, heavy dream. In the dream, he was strong and lean, striding through a spectral forest in big leather boots, tracking giant paw prints. When he wakes up, he's achy and overweight, sprawled on the city couch of an old friend, where he's overstayed his welcome by at least a month.

Chief rolls over and picks up the phone. He's hoping it's Buddy with good news; he left him two messages the day before and two the day before that. But it isn't Buddy on the phone. Instead, it's Droop.

"Hey, I got a van full of crap I need to deliver," Droop says. "You want to take a ride, help me move some crap? I can pay you, like, forty bucks."

"What kind of crap?" Chief asks. Droop, he remembers, was on a moving job he worked a few months before. Droop got fired before lunch. The boss said he couldn't be trusted.

"Nice crap! *Collectible* crap. I buy it and sell it for this lady uptown. I buy it here, I move it there. I'll explain later. I'm on a pay phone."

It doesn't matter what kind of crap it is. Chief has been out of work for weeks, and he needs a refill. He needs the forty bucks.

"Where do you want me to meet you?"

"Don't worry, I know where you live," Droop says. "497 16th, right?"

"That's right," Chief says. Chief doesn't really live here. How does Droop know where he lives?

"Great! I'll swing by in fifteen minutes."

Forty bucks is forty bucks. Chief will call Buddy again later. Chief looks down at the envelope holding his last three pills and pops all three into his mouth. He goes downstairs, the dark hallway's light bulbs streaking past him like light snakes.

An hour later, Droop pulls a battered white van up in front of 497 16th, crunching the side mirror off a Corolla. He pretends not to notice, even though the noise was so loud it stopped a basketball game in the park across the street. Chief climbs in quickly and shakes hands. He remembers Droop more clearly now that he sees him. He has huge puppy eyes that beg people to trust him. His mouth hangs open. The other movers called him "poodle face." They really hated him.

"So I got to stop by this old man first," he says. He swerves and pulls the van out into the middle of the avenue. Something glass cracks behind Chief. A taxi screeches its brakes. Droop pulls out a cigarette and reaches for the lighter.

"So listen. When we see the old man, just tell him you're my partner. All right?"

Droop double-parks in the street, across from a police station. He walks straight up to two policemen wearing knee-high horse boots, leaving his door open, which stops all traffic. "I'm just here for a second, officers," he says to the officers. "I'm just unloading something." The policemen stare at him, then walk back into the station. Droop crosses the street back to his van, then slams the door shut. "I'm talking to the policemen," he shouts at a passing driver who curses him.

Droop waves Chief out. Chief follows him to a green wooden double door splashed with red paint. A single-button buzzer hangs from two fraying wires, one blue and one white, that were pulled out of the wall a long time ago. Droop holds the assembly in one hand and buzzes with the other.

They stand together for two minutes, Droop ringing the bell. Then a voice echoes from somewhere deep inside the building, "I'm coming already!" There's a sound like a rug being dragged across pebbles. Then a bolt turns. Then another bolt turns. The door swings open. An old man with a huge nose wearing a bathrobe glares at Chief, then at Droop. Then he sweeps his arm for them to enter into his darkness.

"This is my partner," Droop says.

"I figured," the old man says.

"How are you doing?" Chief says.

"Been better, partner," the old man says.

The door closes behind them. They stand together at the foot of an old, spindling staircase. A narrow corridor winds behind it into blackness. It is cool in the house. It smells like damp dirt.

The old man gestures for them to follow him down the corridor. He shuffles in old flip-flops beneath dirty white socks, checkered pants that are twice his size, and a rumpled yellow shirt with a huge collar under the bathrobe. He flips a light switch, and a wave of yellow light from a single bulb fills a vast chamber. Lining the walls, leaning on their sides, sitting in crumpled heaps on the floor are the remains of hundreds of stone and wood and steel forms, shapes, human and animal torsos, fat ones and bone-skinny ones, between which lie piles of rumpled clothing, rusting tools, and ancient pieces of furniture. Beyond this room is another room, filled with photographs of human heads behind sculptures that look more or less like the same heads. A quick breath of sunlight slips in somewhere behind a curtain, revealing another room off in the distance.

The old man's face is long and sharp and comes to a perfect point at the end of his nose. He turns and looks at Chief closely for the first time, and it is alarming. His sparkling black eyes seem hopelessly crossed with all that real estate jutting out like a broken sailboat between them. The hairs from his nostrils sparkle like peppered moss. They poke out wildly above the neatly trimmed hint of a mustache, a transom for a row of gray and orange teeth, an overbite, and a receding chin dropping straight down into an old man's neck.

"Are these yours?" Chief asks him.

"Yes, they are."

"What are they?"

"They are piles of crap."

"They're not piles of crap," Droop says. "They're sculptures. Nat's a famous sculptor, aren't you, Nat? You had a show at the museum, didn't you?"

"It was a long time ago," Nat says. "They were fine art then. You know what they are now?" He looks up at Chief.

"What?"

"They're piles of crap."

"They're not piles of crap," Droop says again. "Alice tells me Nat used to hang out with all the famous artists. She said that an artist once traded one of his paintings for Nat's sculptures, and you have it rolled up somewhere. Do you still have that painting he gave you?"

Nat's watching Droop very carefully. He doesn't trust Droop either, Chief thinks.

"Yeah, I got it somewhere," he says. He pauses for a moment. Then he turns and reaches into an umbrella stand behind one of the torsos. Nat slowly unrolls a dry scroll of paper; when it is unrolled, Droop and Chief take a deep breath. It's the most beautiful thing Chief's ever seen, filled with swirling light and color. It's like being deep underwater or deep in outer space, but it's not like that either.

"Here it is," Nat says. "He traded with me for a couple of my pieces. The ones from the museum show. Then he sold them, my sculptures. But I could never bring myself to sell this painting."

"That's worth a lot of money," Droop says. "You know how much money that's worth?"

Nat quickly rolls up the painting, then waves them farther down the corridor. He pulls a dust-covered blanket off an old trunk.

"Did you bring the money?" he asks Droop.

"As agreed," Droop says, pulling out an envelope and counting out six twenties and a five. "One twenty-five."

"We agreed on one seventy-five," Nat says, glaring up at Droop from the corner of one watery eye.

"It was one twenty-five," Droop says. "That's what Alice told me. You can call her if you want to, but she's not home right now. She'll be home tonight. You can call her."

The old man crumples the bills tightly in his little hand. "I'll do that," he says. "I'll call her."

Droop gestures for Chief to take one end of the trunk. It's crushingly heavy, filled with things that are dense and shifting.

"Take it easy," Droop says. He huffs and pants to keep up with Chief as they pull it out through the torsos, to the front door, to the truck. He pulls the latch up; piled in the back are rugs; wooden boxes filled with tarnished jewelry and rusting forties kitchenware; two old dressers and an armoire; and the shattered remains of a vanity mirror. They stuff the trunk in with the boxes and climb back into their seats.

Droop looks back at Nat, who stands in the doorway glaring at them. "Just a minute," Droop says. "I'll be right back." Chief waves at Nat, who doesn't notice him; he squints at Droop, and they disappear through the door. Five minutes later, in the rearview mirror, Chief sees Droop come down the sidewalk, not out the door, with the umbrella stand tucked under his arm. He climbs into the driver's seat, stuffing the umbrella stand quickly behind his seat.

"Why'd you go back?" Chief asks him.

"I had to use his bathroom."

"Why did you come around from the back?"

Droop pulls the van into traffic. "He just sent me out the back door," he says, waving to a cab that's honking, trying to get around. "He's such a pain in the ass. Totally out of his frigging mind. Hey, man, you ever try these?"

Droop pulls a handful of pills, big pink footballs, out of his pocket. Chief grabs a couple and, without thinking, pops them in his mouth. "What are they?" he asks.

"Who knows?" Droop says. Droop pops one and puts the rest in the console between the seats. Instantly, the world beyond the windshield irons itself out, and the taxis and cars drip away from the road in front of them.

Swerving from lane to lane on the avenue, Droop tells Chief all about how much money he's pulling in. Alice, his boss, is a collector. She moves things. She's a monster, he says, and everybody hates her. But she hurt her back, so she hired Droop. She pays him $200 a week to pick up and deliver whatever she's moving and to work her spot at the bazaar on Saturdays. The thing is, Droop's starting to work his own operation on the side; he's starting to meet people, to learn things.

"I picked up another hundred last weekend," he says. "Only a matter of time."

"A matter of time until what?" Chief asks.

"I'm thinking Grizzle," Droop says. "Everybody I used to know is headed up there. You can get a job there working the docks or a cannery or a fishing boat, ten bucks an hour, and sleep in your tent. I just need the cash to get up there, that's all."

"You'll never go to Grizzle," Chief says. "You'll get eaten alive."

"Yeah," Droop says. "You're probably right. Grizzle, Grizzle, Grizzle. Everybody talks about going up there, but nobody ever does. What do you want to go up there for and shiver in the cold? Plenty of money to be made right here."

"I got a friend who went up there a while back," Chief says. "He guides downlanders looking to live off the land. He's hard core, the real deal. He told me he'd show me the ropes if I ever head up there. They call him Hawk."

"Cool! Man, one day. One day I'm gonna call up that guy called Hawk...Hey, was that a Pepsi sign?" Droop pulls the van onto a cross street lined with burned-out apartment buildings and the carcasses of roasted vehicles. Hydrants blow steamy puddles of water out into the streets, but no children are playing in them; the streets are empty. He's looking up at the side of a corner building. A rusted, bent soda fountain sign is hanging by two bolts above a steel grate. Droop slowly pulls the van over but doesn't stop until he butts the front fender into the curb. He climbs out. "Hey, check it out. That's a Pepsi sign. Give me a hand, will you?"

"What are we doing?" Chief asks him. He looks up and down the street. Two big men standing in the next doorway are watching them. Droop opens the back of the van; there's a ladder stuffed in one side. Chief sets up and foots the ladder under the Pepsi sign. Droop climbs up to look at it.

"If it's in good shape," he says. "If there's no rust on the inside...." He says this between pulls, trying to dislodge the bottle cap–shaped sign from the building. Brick dust and rust come down in a cloud on Chief's head. He looks up the street. The two big men are approaching.

"What are you folks doing?" one of them asks.

"I can't get it," Droop says. "Do either of you have a screwdriver or something?"

"You boys with the city or something?"

"Yeah, that's right," Droop says. "We're with the city."

"Because if you aren't with the city," the man continues, "you're ripping something out of our neighborhood."

"We're with the city," Droop says. "A screwdriver? A hammer?"

"You got some papers?" the man asks. Chief looks up the street; two more men are walking toward them.

"In the van," Droop says. He pulls once more, and the sign comes off with a noise like a ringing steel drum. "I'll get them for you."

Droop carries the sign, and Chief carries the ladder. They load them into the back of the van, shut the door, and climb into the front. Droop reaches into the glove compartment and pulls out a pistol. He waves to the men, then turns the key and skids down the street. Then he puts the pistol back in the glove compartment.

"Those Pepsi signs are totally worth it," he says. "If they're in good shape? I can get, like, two hundred bucks apiece."

"I don't think those guys were very happy," Chief says.

"Keep your eyes peeled for those signs," Droop says. "I'll tell you what. When I sell it, I'll split it with you."

Chief follows Droop into the lobby of a huge apartment building. It is evening; a marshy smell rises from the trees in the direction of the river. He leads Chief into a back stairway and down a flight into a boiler room. He props open a steel door with a brick.

"This is how we have to load it all in," he says. "Building management rules. Listen, when we get upstairs…you're just a friend of mine, all right?"

Through an alleyway and back to the street, back and forth, Chief helps Droop carry the trunks, the boxes, the furniture, an ancient brass bed frame, a pair of cracked Tiffany lamps. The Pepsi sign, Droop points out, should stay in the truck. He doesn't mention the umbrella stand. They load the items into a padded service elevator, then ascend to the eighth floor. Droop struggles with a pocketful of keys to open an apartment door. He pushes the door open. Inside is a long hallway leading into a series of rooms. Boxes and disassembled furniture and piles of newspapers and shelves stacked with old books are packed six feet high and three feet deep along each side of the hallway.

An old woman with matted gray hair in a housecoat, reading glasses perched on the edge of a sharp nose, pokes her head out of a kitchen and glares at Chief.

"Who the hell is that?" she asks.

"A friend of mine," Droop says.

While Chief unloads the elevator, dragging each item in and stacking it against the other items in the hallway, Alice pulls Droop into her kitchen and whispers something to him from between her teeth. Something foul is overcooking in an oven somewhere.

Droop waits until Chief unloads most of the contents, then waves him back out into the foyer.

"Um, so," he whispers, "you have to go now."

"Hey," Chief says, suddenly picturing a medicine cabinet. "I got to use the bathroom."

"You can't do that here. Alice is nuts."

"Sure," Chief says, "I understand." But he doesn't move; he stares at Droop, who's growing increasingly uncomfortable.

Droop tries the puppy eyes. "So, um, I'll send you the forty dollars by check. The thing is, Alice doesn't have the cash at the moment. She does everything on the books."

"Oh," Chief says.

"I know where you live though. I got your address. I'll get a check to you at the end of the month. And the Pepsi sign. If I sell it, I'll send you half."

"Right," Chief says. Droop puts out his hand, and Chief shakes it. "You know where I live."

Back out on the street, Chief looks at the van, battered and now almost empty, sitting alone under a streetlamp in front of the building. On his last load up, he never thought to lock it. He opens the driver's-side door, climbs in, and takes the rolled-up painting out of the umbrella stand. Then he reaches into the console and takes the pills. He swallows a handful of them and slides deep into the seat. A blind rage emerges from deep inside of him, but it's separate from his body, a shadow, a strange, shallow light streaking through his veins and up into his arms. He reaches into the glove compartment and removes the pistol. He takes a calming breath. Then he pulls a lamp base out of a last box of broken things behind Droop's seat, and he sits, watching cars streak past in tails of red and white sparklers.

The driver's door opens. Droop jumps in, then instantly realizes his mistake. "Oh, hey again!" he says. "I thought—"

Independent of where he thought the lamp was, Chief watches with a detached fascination as it crosses in an arc in front of him, intermingling with the sparkles outside the windshield, and then makes a dull cracking noise on Droop's forehead. Chief's other arm is already at work, pulling Droop's limp form into the well of the van.

Chief drops the lamp, reaches into Droop's shirt, and pulls four bottles of pills out. He tucks the painting under his arm and stuffs the pistol in his pants. Then he climbs out of the van and walks through the park along the river, into the shadows, quietly chanting, "Grizzle. Grizzle, Grizzle."

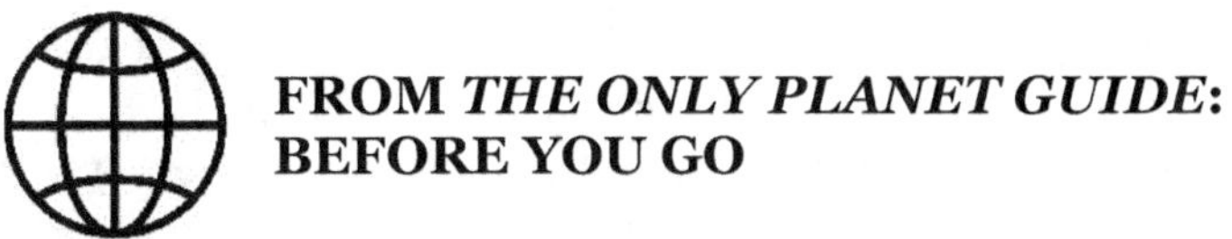

FROM *THE ONLY PLANET GUIDE:* BEFORE YOU GO

Since reopening to travel, each summer sees growing waves of free-spirited backpackers (and Winnebago enthusiasts, hunters, fishermen, and people who think they are going to make a lot of money) winding their way up to the Grizzle Peninsula. Many hearty, adventurous souls who make the journey simply for the sake of the journey itself agree that the trip is worth its weight in gold. For fortune seekers, opportunists, or New Age spiritualists seeking an idyllic convergence of energy, this "gold" will probably prove elusive. The Grizzle Peninsula is spectacular, but it offers no "yellow brick road;" it is more like a hard slog through knee-deep mud.

While some of its wildest legends are the stuff of fairy tales (the best being the legend of the Grizzarillo, probably fabricated by bored army privates; see "Fact versus Fiction" in the "Outer Grizzle, Grizzletown, & The Extremities" chapter), the stories of cold sheets of rain, summer blizzards, bear attacks, swarming insects, hissing fog, volatile volcanoes, quicksand, and trails that lead nowhere are fully substantiated. Evidence of the dangers these conditions create can be found in the government's fast-paced investment in park rangers, fish and game wardens, emergency medical teams, and coastal rescue teams (coastal rescue loses five to six helicopters and their crews in rescue operations each year).

Sadly, people disappear each summer, and they disappear in droves (see the "Outer Grizzle" chapter). It is critical that all travelers, no matter how experienced and how well equipped, come prepared for the unique challenges presented by the Grizzle Peninsula. You don't have to spend a fortune to travel safely in Grizzle, but it is critical that you are ready for everything it can throw at you. Because if you get close enough to the Grizzle Peninsula that it can throw something at you, it will.

A note about employment: Despite rumors to the contrary, there are very few opportunities to make your fortune on the peninsula. There are countless legends of wilderness communes that welcome travelers from down land as laborers and then give them hundreds of dollars to take home with them. Other stories tell of fishing boats recruiting crewmen from the docks and oil companies turning broke hitchhikers into wealthy roughnecks overnight. In truth, employment opportunities have become scarce. The fishing industry, which boomed for several years, busted quickly when huge commercial fishing interests cleaned out the fisheries. Oil and logging companies ship in their workers. The parks department may have positions, but most involve the drudgery of maintaining campgrounds. Trained specialists in medical emergency care, helicopter rescue, firefighting, policing, and fish and game wardens are in steady demand due to the growing numbers of travelers who frequently strand themselves in the wild.

It is still amazing how many people come to the Grizzle Peninsula each year expecting to find streets paved with gold. When locals refer to you as a "downlander" (a mild derogatory) or a "waffle-ass" (much stronger derogatory, evoking the metal mesh benches from the Portia ferry), it is partly because they see summer visitors looking for work as a threat to their meager, hard-fought livelihoods. It is strongly recommended that you come anticipating not to work and accept that you will return home broke.

MAY 1983

FROM THE ONLY PLANET GUIDE: GEOGRAPHY

One testament to the Grizzle Peninsula's wildness is its absolute refusal to allow humans to create a fully accurate topographical map. Aerial photographs of the Grizzle Peninsula are virtually impossible to capture due to the constant shroud of fog and vast expanse of the land itself (and because, until very recently, of military restrictions). Pushed by a deep base of subtectonic plates along the ocean floor some three million years ago, molded first by blasting volcanoes (some of which are still active today) before being split in two by a glacial knife in the last great ice age (creating the Great Gulf), the Grizzle Peninsula is actually a pile of broken rocks, the final push off of the formation of the other great continents. Shoved aside by these huge plates, the Grizzle Peninsula is the geological equivalent of the last piece of crumb cake swept aside by a huge, angry hand.

As made clear from the enclosed foldout map (see map), the Grizzle Peninsula is at its widest where it is cut from the mainland, with approximately one hundred miles of rough, deeply forested terrain between its western and eastern shorelines. Storms beat against the rocky western coastline almost constantly. The eastern coastline, by contrast, slopes gently into a dark blue sea of icy water, frozen over for half the year. It is the eastern coast, for the most part, where the oil lies just off shore. The peninsula's land mass curves almost 1,200 miles, with its trail of high volcanic peaks rising in one long range from the western coastline before dropping abruptly into the great gulf, a canyon dropping almost vertically from the high ledges above. A block of mountainous terrain here splits the peninsula, punctuated by one highly active volcano (last erupting several years ago). Beyond this almost impenetrable region lies Outer Grizzle, a largely unexplored, uninhabitable mass of tangled rocks and shattered forests, all crashing together into the Ledges, the last crumbling cliffs and boulders tumbling into the sea. More than anywhere else, the Ledges—where the western and eastern seas collide—are constantly shrouded in impenetrable fog, tormented by howling winds, and encased in ice and snow, even in summer.

The Ledges have been the end of many a lost boating expedition, doomed flight, and "disappeared" backpacker. It is highly recommended (although the attraction to traverse the entire peninsula is certainly understandable) to stay well clear of the region beyond the Great Gulf.

Danny wakes up
in a tent

Danny wakes up, alone, in a tent. He crawls out into a forest clearing littered with beer cans. The huge belly of a commercial jet lunges up from the dark forest next to him, from an invisible runway, and streaks away. A pickup truck is in front of him, its windows frosted silver with condensation. Tattered blue canvas and fishing gear poking out of the back in all directions. Something curious presses against the passenger-side window. He walks up to take a closer look, then jumps back. It's the face of a sleeping man. His mouth is open, and his cheek, tongue, and most of his beard are stuck to the frosted glass.

Danny turns and hurries down the parking lot to Gretch and the rented car. She sits in the driver's seat, intently reading a map and scratching the back of her head. She looks up at Danny and then quickly back down at the map.

"Well, well, well," she says.

They return to the tent and pack up their gear in silence. Gretch skids out of the parking lot. Danny struggles to think of something to say.

"So how far do you figure it is?" he asks.

"Eight hours," she says.

Gretch pushes the pedal as far down as it goes. She guns the car right up the tail of a logging truck and then swerves around to the other side to pass. She shoots a finger at the driver, then rooster-tails the car back into the center of the long gravel road.

After a long silence, they approach a small settlement. "Say, honey," Gretch says, suddenly and cheerfully, "what do you say we get some gas and some coffee?" She turns into a general store parking lot, splashing an arc of mud and gravel into the woods. "I'll get it," she says, jumping out to pump the gas.

Danny hurries into the general store. He says hello to a tiny ancient woman with hoop earrings who scowls at him from behind the counter. He picks up a box of Cheerios, sees "$7" scribbled on the box top, and drops it on the floor. Replacing it carefully, he moves on until he finds coffee cups next to a dispenser with a sign that reads "self serf." He pushes the dispenser button. Nothing comes out.

"Nothing's coming out," Danny says.

"I just filled it." The woman spits on the floor.

"But nothing's coming out," he says.

"What's the problem," a tiny old man says, stepping from the backroom.

"I just filled it." She spits again.

A tar-like black liquid suddenly spurts out, misses the coffee cup, burns Danny's hand, and lands on the floor. "How much?" he asks.

"Dollar!" she snaps. The two storekeepers stare at Danny with violent hatred in their eyes.

He gives them two dollars, fills two cups, and spills half on the floor on the way out the door. As he walks across the parking lot, Danny takes a full look at Gretch. She is older than he thought. She has piercing blue eyes. She is leaning against the car, examining her map with extra intensity.

She tenses as Danny walks up to her. "Yep, yep, yep," she says, staring up the highway.

In the late afternoon, Gretch and Danny arrive at a public campground. Across from their tent site, a large dredging machine sucks black sludge from the bottom of a river and spits it out onto the far bank. They set up the tent with a view across river, cook dinner at a picnic table, and watch the sludge pile grow.

They share a six-pack as the midnight sun floats down toward the distant horizon. The dredging machine shuts down, and its noise is replaced by the steady drone of mosquitoes and the rumble of camper generators from nearby campsites. As she brushes bugs away, Gretch tells Danny about her surveying work and mentions something about watershed management. He asks her what watershed management is. She uses her hands to draft water down imaginary slopes and into underground currents. Then she tells him about tundra and permafrost and the Mubbles along the eastern coast—thermal-heated towers of rainbow-colored mud that spout into the air and glow at night. She asks him questions about the park ranger training program he's signed up for that starts in a week. They are starting to get along just fine, Danny thinks. The awkwardness is lifting. Everything is going to be okay. He climbs into his side of the tent, and then she climbs into hers, and they say good night. Just as he drifts off to sleep, Gretch leans over and puts her arm across his chest. "Good night, sweetie," she says. Danny freezes. He keeps his eyes sealed shut. After a minute, she rolls back over to her side of the tent.

The next morning they have breakfast at a diner on the side of the highway. A pair of truckers at the counter tease the waitress, an old woman with blue hair. "You shut your lip, darling," she says.

Danny smiles across the Formica table at Gretch. "What are you looking for?" he asks cheerfully.

She frowns up at him, then looks back down at the maps and geological surveys she has spread across the table. "Permafrost," she says.

*

At the entrance to the Great Gulf Wilderness Park, there is a visitor center with a backcountry permit desk. On the way in, Gretch turns to Danny with a panicked look on her face.

"Listen, just don't say nothing about the surveying stuff, okay? We're just backpackers, that's all."

At the desk, as Gretch fills out a backcountry hiking permit, two park rangers shake their heads and make grave warnings. "You should really consider staying on the Great Gulf Trail," a ranger tells Danny. "There's a great campsite up there, real spectacular site. If weather rolls in, we'll know where to find you."

Gretch rolls her eyes and insists, again and again, that she knows all about weather and bear encounters and wild, raging rivers and summer blizzards. Worn down, the rangers fall silent and give them a receipt, bear-proof food canisters, permits, and maps.

As they drive the rental car up a logging road, high into the backcountry, it starts to rain. The road ends in front of a wide river rushing out of a steep mountain gorge. They follow a trail for several hundred yards that soon becomes a goat trail, and then no trail at all. The footing is wet and spongy. Climbing across a steep ledge, they come to a wall of spruce thickets eight feet tall.

Gretch stares into the tangled jungle and then turns to Danny, grinning. "What do you say we just bull our way through, honey? Huh? What do you say?" She disappears into the thicket, cracking branches.

Danny follows, quickly losing sight of her. The branches tangle and twist around him, shoving him back as he pushes forward. The air is thick and humid and acrid with rotting vegetation. Finally Danny brakes out on what appears to be a steep mudslide, the river gorging thousands of feet below. Gretch stands before him, panting, ankle deep in mud and water. Leaves and branches stick out from her backpack, from her boots, from under her hat. Her face is covered with welts, and water trickles down from her ears.

"Hey, Gretch," Danny says. "What do you say we work our way down to the river, try working along the coastline? Won't be so tough through there. What do you think?"

"Now that's just ridiculous," she says in a voice that is both calming and ridiculing. "We just have to stick with this game plan, bull our way through." She sucks her boots out of the mudslide and plunges into the next green wall. They push into the forest four times, emerging each time onto a new mud slick. They slowly but steadily pass beneath stark mountain ledges and into the basin of the Great Gulf. At the far end, Danny follows Gretch up and over a ledge of slippery rock. A long valley spreads out before them. Out in the open, a rainy, stark wind whistles through Danny's wet rain gear.

They set up camp on a ragged ledge beneath a stone buttress. Danny cooks dinner a half-mile from the tent, keeping a wary eye out for bears. Gretch yells above the din of the wind, "We shoulda camped up there on the peak. Look!" He stares up and sees nothing but dangling ledges, snow ravines, and shrubs clinging for dear life. "I'm good and scared right here, thanks," he yells back. She shakes her head and looks away. Suddenly a sunbeam breaks through the clouds and paints a section of the valley floor beneath them in a spectrum of chrome greens and silvers as it reflects off the wet tundra. The first beam closes, and two more follow, moving up the cliff walls around them. They sit for an hour, both in their own worlds. Then the clouds seal the sun away, and darkness blankets the valley.

For three days Gretch leads Danny on a silent trek crossing ravines and mountain ridges, pushing through waist-deep freezing water and dense overgrowth. They cross fresh paw prints, hear wolves howling at the moon, and follow mountain sheep across steep ledges. They stop only for Gretch to set up her surveying tools, jot notes in a notebook, and fold everything up. On the third morning, they push back through the gulf. As they catch sight of the logging road and rental car, Gretch speaks.

"Well, I guess you only got a couple more days of freedom."

"Yeah," Danny says. "It won't be so bad."

"Well, I'm thinking of driving down to Can-Town and checking it out. What do you say? I haven't been back there since my fishing days. We'll have some fun. Then I'll drive up to Petrolia and drop you off at the airport for the trip up to your training or whatever. What do you say, honey?"

"Sounds great," Danny says.

In Can-Town, a long stretch of sand peeks out into a wide harbor, with fishing shacks, bars, docks, and boats all clinging to a wide strip of asphalt. Pickup trucks swerve across either side of the road, drunks whooping out the passenger windows. Danny helps Gretch pitch her tent on the beach, near a series of home-rigged plywood and tarpaulin shacks. As they walk back to the road, they get menacing looks from long-faced men poking sticks into campfires. They pick up a six-pack and go to the long row of docks to look at the fishing boats. They walk by rows of fish hanging from hooks, flayed and flapping in the wind. They sit on a jetty, watching the sun slowly drop behind a volcano across the harbor. They finish the beers and start back to the tent.

"So, the surveying thing," Danny says. "Who do you work for?"

"Why do you want to know?"

"Nothing. Just curious."

"Hey, what do you say?" Gretch says, her face lighting up. "It's the Salty Dawg! Let's go in for a beer, huh? Farewell beer? What do you say, huh?"

Danny looks up at a fake lighthouse propped above the short black building.

"Sure," he says. "Why not."

Inside, a long, dark oak bar faces three picnic tables. A middle-aged woman in a blond wig and a white blouse tends bar, wiping glasses with a rag. Two fishermen sit by the door, staring into their beers. A large bear of a man sits slouched on a stool in the middle of the bar, talking to the bartender.

"Like I saying," the big man says after Gretch and Danny order two beers and sit down at a picnic table, "how come you never smile, Donna? Smile, just for me."

"No," Donna says.

"Come on, just once." He shifts his belly on his lap. A fresh pink cut gapes across the bridge of his nose. "Hey, fellers," he says down the bar to the two smaller fishermen sitting by the door. "She ever smile? Ever?"

"No, Bob," one of the two men says. "Never."

"Bet you're real pretty when you smile," Bob says.

"Do you believe what an a-hole that guy is?" Gretch says loudly. Her words bounce off the back wall of the bar. The two fishermen at the door hold their beers halfway between the bar and their mouths. Gretch turns to Donna. "Don't see why you have to put up with that crap, sister," she bellows, her face turning red. "That guy's a grade-A jerk." She jumps up and sits at the bar, two seats from Bob.

The two fishermen put down their beers and get up. "Good night, Donna," they say and push out the door. Bob runs a fat finger over the rim of his beer mug.

"Well, come on up here, hon, what do you say!" Gretch waves Danny up to the bar. He pulls up on a stool between Bob and Gretch and orders a beer.

"So, Donna, what do you say I beat the crap out of this guy?" Bob thumbs at Danny. "Will that make you smile?"

"Will nothing, Bob," Donna says. "Don't start no trouble."

Gretch smashes her beer mug down on the bar. "That's telling him, sister!"

Bob turns to Danny. "What are you looking at?" He points at Danny with a dirty black finger.

"I'm not looking at anything," Danny says.

"You looking at me, waffle ass?"

"You know what?" Danny asks him. He smiles, and he leans up into Bob's face. "You're a pretty funny guy!" As he says it, he hops off his stool and moves straight for Bob. Bob reaches out for Danny's neck with his far hand, but misses. Danny dodges around him for the door. As Bob lunges, the stool falls backwards, and he falls with it. As Danny swings the bar door open, he hears Bob crash to the floor behind him. In a second, Danny is out from under the parking lot streetlights and into the safe twilight darkness of the beach.

Down the beach, Gretch catches up with Danny and says, "Well, that was chicken crap."

Danny looks at her and realizes she's grinning, for real, for the first time on the whole trip.

Fiona in the
Mubbles

Fish and Game Cadet Fiona Gallagher sits on the rickety steps of a Quonset hut, blowing steam off a cup of instant coffee from her camp stove. She's watching the sun rise through strips of fog that brush vertically over the surface of a glassy harbor. A circle of old-growth pines ascends into shimmering metallic grasses clinging to steep cliffs that rise to snowfields, and then the sky. As the sun comes up, the glimmering water ripples and shines, silver and blue, green and brown.

Fiona squints, trying to find the spot on the horizon where the sea ends and the sky begins. She remembers a creased and dog-eared photograph her brother Freddie sent her some years ago. In the photo she could make him out, just barely, standing on a crop of rock just above the same harbor. She lost the photo a while back, with everything else, back there, before she came up here. She can't decide if this was the same place in the photo, or if Freddie was the person standing on the rock, or if he sent a picture of somebody else standing on the rock, or if there ever was a picture at all.

This morning everything is still. For the prior two days, a storm raged from the sea, bringing forceful winds and sheets of freezing rain down here, and summer snow in the higher elevations. But now the storm has blown over, and this morning is the last day of her training cycle. At the end of the day, she'll be assigned, and then flown out by helicopter in the morning to her new life.

Fiona rose early, hoping to drink in one last morning of this place that has transformed her, and hardened her, and maybe cured her of something she needed to be cured of.

For a few seconds, Fiona observes as the cove where she sits goes stone-cold quiet—no lapping waves, no wind in the pines, no seagulls—and then just as suddenly, it erupts into a cacophony of noise. A radio cackles in one of the other huts. A seaplane buzzes from behind the cliffs. A great breath of wind blows a thick cloud through a gap in the mountains. From up the beach, Fiona can hear Bucket-Hat's boots squeaking in the sand, coming up the beach, even though he's still a hundred yards away. Something's up, Fiona thinks. She finishes her coffee, hides the mug, and laces up her boots.

"Something's up, Cadet," Bucket-Hat announces between deep pants from the long walk through the sand. "The Captain needs you. I'd go, but I gotta man the radio," he says, scratching the back of his long neck. "I'd go," he repeats for emphasis, "but you don't know how to man the radio."

I know how to man the radio better than anybody here, Fiona thinks to herself. I aced that test, and you know it. I can take your radio apart and put it back together with a popsicle stick. But she doesn't say anything; she's still a cadet. Bucket-Hat ranks above her, and the Captain far above Bucket-Hat. In Fish and Game, she learned early in her training, rank means everything. You do as you are told inside this world, and you'll have total authority outside this world.

Fiona follows Bucket-Hat around the bend of the shoreline, through the all-too-familiar clump of felled logs, and into the headquarters hut. The Captain sits at his desk, struggling to clip a pile of paperwork into a binder. He lets them both stand there a moment. Fiona is perfectly still; Bucket-Hat is breathing heavily, wiping sweat from his forehead with a handkerchief.

"Good morning, Cadet," the Captain says.

"Good morning, Captain."

"So I know this is officially your last day, and we're supposed to just wrap you up in paperwork and send you on your merry way, but we have a little problem that you might be able to help us with."

"Whatever it takes, sir."

"It appears that our visitor has disappeared," the Captain says. "The hippie feller. The Bear Man. You've no doubt seen him wandering around camp."

Fiona had noticed him a few days before—a wizard hat and robe, long hair, long beard, barefoot. Between exams on fishing and hunting permits and regulations, orientation training, survival training, firearms training, and marching fifteen to twenty miles a day with full gear—she hardly noticed anything. But she definitely noticed the Bear Man.

"I have, yes."

"He just bummed a ride in on a chopper and showed up one day," Bucket-Hat says, removing his bucket hat to reveal a surprisingly bald head. "I asked him what he was doing, and he told me he was clan-master of the Bear Institute and he was here to talk to the bears. He said he done heard them speaking to him in his dreams, and they would meet him at the Mubbles, and he would lead them to a safe place, out past the Extremities, and they would establish a bear kingdom there, and he would be their king, clan-master of the bears, and he was already clan-master of the bears, and why don't I just mind my own business. So I said, 'Sure, don't be sore, no hard feelings,' and I went back to my post." Bucket-Hat pulls his hat back on, tugging it over his ears. "I guess in hindsight, I could of been more assertive."

"Cadet, we can't get a helicopter up there, we've got nothing until tomorrow, and there's weather coming in. I need you to go out to the Mubbles and see if you can find him and get him back here safe. If you have to, arrest him."

"Yes, sir."

"And take a rifle."

"Yes, sir. Is he considered a threat?"

"That hippie? No. But there are some mean bears up there. And it's tricky terrain. Watch your step in the Mubbles. Use your instincts and your training, and you'll be okay. And Cadet?"

"Yes, sir?"

The Captain looks out the cabin window at a chopper sitting idly in the clearing.

"The day you climbed off the chopper four weeks ago, I almost turned you around and sent you straight back to whatever downland hellhole you climbed out of. You didn't look like you would last a day. Every other cadet who climbed off that chopper looked like a winner, but none of them could take it. None of them lasted two weeks. This place breaks people, but it didn't break you." The Captain reaches into his drawer and pulls out a small badge. He hands it to Fiona. "I got no idea what you got inside of you that drove you to want to do this line of work, but whatever it is, you've got what it takes. You're ready for this."

"Thank you, sir."

"No need to thank me, Cadet. You earned it. Now go out there and find that hippie."

The mud bubbles; the mumbling mud bubbles. Everybody just calls it the Mubbles. The forest service trail that runs from the old base up to the Mubbles climbs slowly and steadily to the gap. With everything she needs on her back and a rifle in her hand, Fiona feels coiled, wary but confident in her training and her newfound physical abilities. She runs through possible scenarios in her head and checks off the list of regulations in her head—how to persuade reluctant and unpermitted visitors to leave unsafe situations, how and when to call for backup, how to track lost visitors, how to recover a body.

Several miles in, the sun breaks through the roof of the white birch forest she's been traversing, illuminating the tree trunks and boulders and shattered branches all around her in a glowing yellow light. Fiona's mind wanders briefly to all of the elements that brought her here and submerges any thoughts of what she left behind. She is here now. She understands why she's here. She understands why Freddie had wanted her to come up here. She didn't understand then, but she understands now. She doesn't let sad thoughts sink into her system, pull her back down the hill. She's climbing a hill, slow but steady. Her legs are like pistons. Her shoulders bear the weight. Her lungs fill with air. She forgets what time is. She forgets the scenarios, the training, the regulations. She breathes the cool air in, and she blows it out. Her mind grows more and more silent as four miles pass beneath her feet.

The forest floor stops where the cliffs begin, a series of vertical rock faces that she will scramble up into the gap, which will bring her to the Mubbles. Fiona stops just long enough to strap the rifle she's been carrying onto her pack. With her hands, she pulls herself up between two boulders and then scrambles on all fours up a rockslide. It doesn't take long for the rocks to curve backward into the mountain. Soon Fiona is standing in the gap looking back at the cove and the silvery sea behind it, the circle of volcanic peeks curving off into the forever. She turns and looks into a dark valley, brushed with fresh snow. There's a packed wall of stunted pine trees and, just beyond them—held between steep snow-streaked cliffs like they are cupped in a monstrous rocky hand—the steaming brown-and-green pools belching steamy smoke rings into the sky.

Fiona pulls the rifle back, double-checks it, and takes it in her hand. Then she descends into the woods. At the edge of the forest, something stops her. The trees are knotted, tangled pine bushes, twisted into each other from the harsh winds, with only the faint sign of a trail within them. They are laced with summer snow and ice from the two-day storm; wind-swept drifts six feet high, six feet deep, are packed between the trees. Fiona pushes through the first snow bank and then another, the deep tangle of trees closing around her. And it's the smell. The smell that traps her. It traps her in a memory she wasn't expecting. She's been fighting remembering anything, but with this particular deep, drunken pine smell, she can't fight it; she buries her head into a snowy branch and drinks the deepest possible draft of that smell.

When Fiona was fourteen and Freddie was eleven, they traveled for their last Christmas together to their Uncle Pete's farmhouse. When they showed up from the bus stop, he was drunk and clearly had forgotten that he had invited them. He had made up a whole big story about all of their aunts and uncles and cousins coming together to see them. When they looked into the house, they saw him lying on a couch, watching a football game. He answered the door in his pajamas, holding a beer.

"Can we come in?" she asked him. "We walked all the way from the bus stop. Freddie's freezing."

"Tell you what," Uncle Pete said. "I have to pull the house together a little. I'll take your bags, but, um, hey. Here's ten bucks. Why don't you guys go buy a Christmas tree? And when you come back, we can all decorate it. All your aunts and uncles will be here by then." He shut the door.

"Freddie's freezing," she said to the door, but it was no use. When they walked out to the street, she looked back. He was already lying down on the couch again, watching the game.

They walked into town. Snowflakes started swirling around them, the wind straight in their faces. Nobody was selling trees.

"Where are we going to find a tree?" Freddie, red-faced, asked.

"Oh, we'll find a tree," Fiona said.

Just then an old man in a huge, fur-lined snorkel jacket emerged from one of the alleyways, dragging a shovel.

"Excuse me, sir!" Fiona said.

"What are you kids doing out here without hats on your heads?" the old man said.

"I wonder if you might direct me to a place where I might purchase a Christmas tree, sir."

The old man wiped his nose with the back of a padded mitten.

"It's fourteen degrees out today, kids," he said. "You go home now, and you tell your mom and dad to get you a hat. Only a damned fool would send their kids out here without a hat on your head."

"Thank you, sir," Fiona said. They kept walking.

"Boy, what a grouch," Freddie said.

"This town is stupid," Fiona said. "This is a stupid town."

"Where are we going to find a tree?"

A station wagon drove around the corner. A large green tree was strapped to the roof. Two little children, hoods snapped around their faces, stared at them through the rear passenger window. Freddie smiled and waved eagerly at the kids. They didn't wave back.

"I know where to go now," Fiona said, following the tracks. "I know where to find a tree."

They followed the tire tracks for another mile through blowing snow. Then they found it, a little farm stand with three Christmas trees leaning up against a horizontal two-by-four. One tree was twelve feet tall, the others only five feet. A sign read, "Half-Price Special All Day."

"I want the big one," Freddie chattered.

"Hello, sir!" Fiona yelled to a man inside a little wooden shed. A space heater glowed behind him. He was bundled in a snorkel jacket.

"What," the man said, scratching his beard.

"I wonder if you could tell me how much for the big tree, sir."

"I don't care. Ten bucks."

Fiona reached with her stinging red fingers and managed to pull out the crumpled bill.

"Here's ten dollars," she said.

"Good. Now I can go home," the man said. He pulled a bundle of string and a huge knife from the shed. "Where's your car?"

"Car?"

"Yeah. Your *car*, girl. How did you get here?"

"We walked, sir. From the town."

"That's very far. It's going to snow two foot. You know that?"

"Maybe we can rig something up, sir. With the string, I mean." The man cut the string, pulled the shed door closed, and locked it. He handed her the string.

"Hey, I don't care what the hell you do with it," he said. "It's your tree now." He climbed into a pickup truck and drove out of the parking lot, turning toward town.

An hour later they were still dragging the big tree through the snow, lost. The snow was billowing in great blasts, down into their shoes, pants, and collars. It no longer mattered, really, because they were so focused on carrying, then dragging, then pushing the huge Christmas tree down the middle of the slippery road.

Exhausted, they sat down in the bows of the tree, which enveloped them, sheltering them from the wind and the snow. Fiona pulled one of the tube socks off her hand; it was soaked and plastered with particles of ice. "Maybe we should give up on the tree or something?" she said.

But this is what she remembers as she inhales the sweet pine into her nostrils, her lungs—it was little brother who said, "No way we're giving up now, big sister." Freddie took Fiona's frozen hands in his, and they rubbed them together. They were inside that tree, held within its branches; the wind and snow piling up outside in drifts, sheltering them. "We made it this far. We're getting this tree back to that house."

"Maybe the aunts and uncles and cousins are already there," Fiona said. "Maybe they're thinking, 'When are they going to get here with that tree?'"

"It's really warm in here," Freddie said. "One day I'm going to build a tree house, just like this. And I'm going to live there. And big sister, you can come live there too. We'll both live in a tree."

Fiona knew they should get moving, but they stayed there, dozing in that cozy little Christmas tree cave on the side of the street, until the cave filled with the warm glow of headlights.

"Uncle Pete! Aunt Rosie! Uncle Charlie!" Freddie yelled.

But the headlights belonged to a squad car. The policeman took them to the empty house, then to the bar where they found Uncle Pete. Fiona and Freddie spent their last Christmas together in a police station. The policeman bought them a pizza, and the old lady from welfare brought them hats and mittens. After that incident, the state shipped Fiona and Freddie off and split them up for real.

Here, twelve years later, in a mountain pass thousands of miles away, Fiona allows herself one last, deep draft of a pine tree in the snow, and then she pushes off.

"Wow, Freddie," she says. "I'll tell you something, little brother—I can still smell that Christmas tree."

There is another gradual climb through the stunted pine tree forest before the Mubbles present themselves, a glowing lake of bubbling mud and steam hissing in a ring of snow and ice cliffs. Dead tree stumps, petrified, stick up from the burning muck. The place smells of sulfur and something organic. Fiona stops on the rocky lip, surveying the landscape. The checklist she started creating in her head at the outset of the trip comes back to her. *What am I looking for? What is here that shouldn't be here?*

Scanning the surroundings, her eyes settle on a glint of something purple that seems out of place, more for its shape than color. A speck, really, but she knows instantly that it shouldn't be here. Climbing over fallen logs, careful not to set foot in the sucking, bubbling mud, she approaches the item carefully. It is a robe, or a cape, neatly folded and tucked squarely into a branch. As she gets closer, she thinks she hears singing—a high-pitched, squeaky kind of singing, coming from somewhere below the tree.

"Coming in," she says. She looks over the last log. And there, lying flat on his back, is a six-foot-tall man with long black hair and a beard, completely naked, in a pool of steaming mud and milky green water.

"Greetings," the Bear Man says. "I can explain. You see, I'm here to speak with the bears, but we've had some issues. I'm giving them the day to think it over, and while here, I decided I needed a good, hot bath."

"I'm going to turn away," Fiona says, "just long enough for you to get out of that pool and get your clothes on."

"Yes," the Bear Man says, "but as you can see, there's a problem. When I got into the pool, I washed my robes and folded them up there to dry, but then a storm came in and they froze." The Bear Man pulls his beard out of the water, examines it, and brushes mud from it like it's a necktie. "If I climb from this pool, I'll be frozen solid in five minutes. So, as you can see, I'm in quite a dilemma."

Without taking her eyes off the Bear Man, Fiona reaches into her pack, pulls out her sweater and a space blanket, and places them on the log. "You've got one minute," she says. "Get dressed, and we're going."

"But what about my bears?"

"Your bears?"

"Yes. I mean, I'm expecting them back any minute."

"You need to come with me, now, back to headquarters," Fiona says. "If the bears need you, they'll know where to find you."

Barefoot, with the sweater and the space blanket wrapped around himself like a shawl, the Bear Man moves slowly through the forest, across the gap, and down the cliff to the birch forest. Long shadows move through the woods, and another bank of dark clouds builds up above the sea. The Bear Man chatters senselessly the whole way down. He is relieved, he says, and grateful; if Fiona hadn't come for him, he might have starved. His bear friends are lovely but very temperamental, he says; they never share their food. Fiona remains silent, ten paces behind the Bear Man, and doesn't let her gun down for a moment.

The Bear Man enters a clearing ahead of her. As soon as she steps into the space, she senses a presence.

"Stop moving," she says to the Bear Man in a low but clear voice.

The Bear Man stops and looks at her. "Whatever do you mean?" he asks.

The bear, a large male, rises. It is standing thirty feet to the Bear Man's left, over a fresh moose kill. This bear is staring at the Bear Man. It makes a quick yipping noise.

"You need to turn around and face the bear," Fiona says in her low voice, quietly raising the rifle under her arm, "but don't make eye contact. You need to speak in a low voice, calmly. You need to hold your ground."

Fiona moves, very slowly, toward the Bear Man. She is never going to get there. Freddie, what do I do? What I'm trained to do? What I want to do? She pulls the gun up. The safety clicks. The bear cocks its head and growls.

"Don't be ridiculous!" the Bear Man says, sitting down cross-legged and smiling at the bear. "The bears love me! I'm their leader. I'm going to sing to the bear!"

Fiona, fully on autopilot now, watches as the Bear Man starts singing loudly in a high-pitched soprano voice, beckoning for the bear to come to him.

"Here, darling, come to me. Come to me, my darling..."

The bear—easily a six hundred–pounder, Fiona estimates—doesn't hesitate. Springing from its back legs, it uncoils and bolts straight for the Bear Man, who suddenly stops singing.

And when the bear gets within ten feet of Bear Man—and when all hopes of a bluff charge are off the table—Fiona does what she is trained to do.

Chief follows Hawk into
the wilderness

Huffing, sweating, and cursing, Chief follows his old friend Michael "Hawk" Hawkins into the wilderness. They walk ten miles on the first day, following an unmarked trail deeper into a forest. Chief trails Hawk over slippery roots, through overgrown branches, and across freezing streams sputtering with glacial runoff from the distant mountains. Other than a few clearings filled with rusting cans, a rotting tent platform, and the skeleton of an ancient jeep, there are no signs of human life. Finally, the trail opens onto a lake ringed with pine trees. Orange streaks of light spill from the sky. Chief puts his pistol back in its holster, drops his pack, and lies down.

"Looks as good a place as any," Hawk says, waving a cloud of mosquitoes away with his floppy hat. "Man, am I starving."

Sitting on a log, Hawk pulls a rust-flecked camp stove from his pack and struggles to assemble it, cursing each part. He then pulls six little packages of ramen noodles out of a stuff sack.

"What are those?" Chief asks.

"Those are the dinners."

"They're awfully small," Chief says, staring at the packages.

"They expand," Hawk says, pumping and lighting the stove. He fills a pot with water, crunches up one of the noodle packets, and dumps it in the pot. He rips open the little soup packet and pours it in. He puts the lid on the pot, lets it boil for a few minutes, and opens the lid. Inside the pot is a little pile of brown noodles simmering in a half-inch of broth. Hawk pours half into his pot and hands Chief the other. Chief wolfs his down in three bites.

"Is that dinner?" Chief asks.

Hawk holds up the wrapper. "It looks different here on the package." He points to the picture of steaming vegetables and meat and pounds of noodles. "It says, 'serves two.'"

"That's a 'serving suggestion' picture," Chief says.

"Look, man. It's the perfect backcountry food. It doesn't weigh anything."

"So you brought six of those? Those are the dinners?"

"Yeah," Hawk says.

They are quiet for a long time.

"It's not so bad," Hawk finally says. "It's only, like, eighty miles to Portia. We can resupply in Portia. I know some people there. And I brought a ton of granola, and you got that gun there. And our stomachs will shrink in a few days. We'll need less food. You'll see."

Stars appear in the sky. Ripples roll across the surface of the lake. A huge moose head rises out of the water, wet leaves and reeds tangled up in its antlers. The moose blinks up at them for a second, chews, then sinks back down into the water.

The second day, Chief follows Hawk through a stretch of forest burned out in a recent forest fire. The land is littered with charred logs and trunks. Huge, dead skeleton trees reach out and grab at Chief. Hawk disappears ahead. At midday, Chief finds him sitting on a log on the side of a dirt road.

"What's for lunch?" Chief asks.

Hawk pulls out his bag of granola. Before hiking out in the morning, he'd pulled the same bag out for breakfast. The bag looks a lot smaller than it did in the morning. They look ahead at a dark, tangled forest.

"Well, here goes," Hawk says. He gets up and plunges ahead. Chief follows him.

In a few steps, the world changes. The woods are dark and clogged with tangled branches and vines. The ground is soft and damp and laced with tangled roots and sharp rocks. Water bubbles everywhere from gurgling streams. Tripping and sliding on the wet surface, Chief can barely follow Hawk's backpack, moving farther and farther away. After many hours, he bursts into a little clearing. A fire is burning in a pile of rocks. Hawk is lying on his back, his pack thrown to one side, his wet socks and boots thrown to another.

"Time for dinner," Hawk says, jumping up. He dumps a packet of ramen noodles into the pot. They eat in fast slurps, burning their mouths. They lick the pots. They put them down and lie down on their sleeping bags, holding their stomachs.

"How long does eighty miles take?" Chief asks.

"I don't know," Hawk says. "We did twelve miles today. So maybe six days. We should get there in four, five more days."

"But we've only got four more of those noodle things," Chief says.

"We got the granola, all right?" Hawk holds up the half-empty bag.

"We can't resupply. There's no stores out here. You told me that. Right?"

"Yeah, well, that's a minor technicality."

"Technicality? If we keep going, aren't we going to starve to death?"

Hawk scratches angry red bug bites on his neck. "Look, man, you needed to disappear, right? If the law's looking for you, the law's looking for you. And besides, where we're headed, you're going to need to forage for your own food, right? So that's what the gun is for, I hope. And besides that, it's my estimation that food is overrated. Once your stomach shrinks, you won't be so hungry."

Day three melds into day four. The trail cuts into a marsh. They ford a number of deep, swollen streams. The rain turns heavier, the mud thicker. By the late afternoon of day four, Chief, stumbling, is daydreaming, first about pills, and then about an ice-cold beer. The beer is in a bottle, pulled from an old icebox. It's so cold it makes his teeth hurt. He becomes so wrapped up in the fantasy that he walks straight into the back of Hawk, who's standing at the base of a pile of shattered rock climbing up into the clouds. Hawk pulls out the granola bag.

"Whaddaya say?" Hawk asks. "Another handful?"

Chief looks at Hawk. He's starting to look a little crazy; sticks and vines poke out of his tangled hair. His hands are black, and he nibbles nervously on the stale crumbs. Chief takes the bag; there is less than a handful left.

They climb up the steep side of the mountain, one hand over the other, between bleached shrubs and mossy rocks. Suddenly the trees give way. They stand in blinding sunlight on top of a huge, rounded blue boulder. Chief rubs his eyes. The entire top of the mountain shines blue.

He panics—he's delirious. Then his eyes focus. "Blueberries!" he yells. Huge, fat blueberries spread out in clumps on bushes across the entire summit of the mountain. Hawk's already stuffing his mouth. Chief joins him. He pulls an empty plastic bag out of a side pocket and starts filling it. They keep stuffing their mouths. They gorge themselves. They eat until they're sick.

The blueberry bushes spread in clumps, hanging from little rock shelves at the top of the mountain. On the top shelf, a bald scrape of rock in the sky, Chief looks back and can barely make out a little gray rectangle of a mountain pass where the road was, where they started walking four days ago. Below him a dark green forest spreads out, with lakes glistening in the late afternoon sun. Chief then looks in the other direction, and his heart sinks. All he can see is a thousand splintered gray mountains beneath a wall of clouds.

They stumble down the far side of the mountain and find the next clearing. They put the bag of blueberries in the creek, planning to keep them cold and eat them over the next four days. But after another little dinner of ramen noodles, they return to the blueberries. Now they are ice cold, like blueberry ice cream.

"How much farther to Portia?" Chief asks, digging his fingers into the bag and scooping up another handful.

"A few days," Hawk says. "When we get there, I know some people I want you to meet. They got a little camp on the outskirts of town. They can show you the ropes."

"I thought you were going to show me the ropes."

"Who, me? No, man. I'll hang for a bit, but I'm moving on to Grizzletown. I got some people I got to see."

"Why don't I come with you?"

"Because you'll never make it is all," Hawk says, pulling his floppy hat down over his eyes. He picks up the blueberry bag, zips it shut, and stares at it for a second. Then he unzips it and pours the entire contents in his mouth. "Ah, well," he says. "Plenty more where those came from."

Then Hawk takes a dozen pine needles, twists them up tightly in one hand, and reaches into his pack with the other.

"You gotta have faith, man," he says. "There's plenty more blueberry patches up ahead. I know it. And we got some food left. And when we run out, we'll find more. We'll scrounge. We'll bum it off people."

"Yeah," Chief whispers. "Scrounge. Bum."

"Last time I came up here, the trail was still packed with ice. I had to crawl through half of it. That time I took, what? Four boxes of mac and cheese and a box of Cheerios. It took me two weeks."

"Mac and cheese," Chief says.

"Yeah. But the thing with mac and cheese is, you need butter and milk. I didn't know that. So I had it straight up. Watery cheese powder and white noodles. Plus I ran out of stove fuel and couldn't light a fire, so I had to chew it raw. I spent the whole trip doubled over with the cramps."

"How long ago was that?"

"I don't know," Hawk says. "I forget." He pulls a piece of toilet paper out of the pack, rolls the pine needles tightly into the paper, and puts the end in his mouth. He reaches in again and pulls out his matches.

"You're not going to smoke that, are you?"

Hawk shakes the matchbox, then puts it away.

"No, man. These are pine needles. What do you think? You think I'm going to smoke pine needles?"

The fifth morning, Chief picks up the Ziploc bag that held the blueberries they collected the night before. Only two remain, crushed, bleeding purple against the plastic. Chief rolls up the bag and stuffs it into a side pocket.

They push off, hungrier than before. Chief has to stop regularly to pull his shorts up, which keep sliding down his backside. It rains, then stops. They slog through more mud. At noon, they stop for a little handful of Cheerios.

"Not looking too good," Hawk says, licking his fingers.

Toward the end of the day, their heads hanging low, they come to a sign pointing to a blue blazed trail: Black Antlers Camp 0.6 miles.

The forest opens up. They walk out onto a little sandy peninsula with a few dilapidated cabins and a couple of trees; the land juts out into the middle of a huge mountain lake spread out under a sheet of low-hanging clouds.

They roll out their sleeping bags on the floor of the cabin with a partial roof. They walk down to the beachfront to cook their dinner.

Hawk dumps the noodles into the pot. Chief hears a motor somewhere far away. Hawk raises his head from the ground. A boat is crossing the lake. The buzzing grows louder. A little boat comes to a halt on the other side of the sandbar.

Two big men climb out of the boat. Fishing things hang out of pockets on their vests. Big moustaches hang from their faces. They dump things from the boat out onto the beach—crates, barrels, stuff sacks. They drag their boat and their gear from the beach up onto the grass.

"Hey there!" Chief yells.

"Hey!" the men yell in unison, surprised, then turn back to their business.

Hawk dumps half the contents of the pot into the lid and hands it to Chief. As they slurp down the noodles, they stare as the big ones unfold a huge four-burner Coleman stove. The men clean a dozen glistening fish, slather them in butter, boil up a big pot of instant mashed potatoes, and stir a brown powder into a side pot.

"That's the gravy," Hawk says.

"Huh."

"It's instant. Instant gravy."

"I'm gonna go catch a fish," Chief says.

"Instant gravy and spuds," Hawk says.

Chief runs up to his pack and digs out the little fishing hook and line he'd tucked into a side pocket. He strings the line to a stick, places a piece of smushed blueberry onto the hook, and casts it into the lake.

"Yes, sir," Chief says.

"Spuds and fish and gravy," Hawk says, lying down on the beach, holding his stomach. The wind is now coming across the sandbar, and the smell of grilled fish surrounds them.

Chief casts again.

"Any day now," he says.

One of the big ones gets up and walks toward them.

"What do you think he wants?" Chief says.

"Maybe he wants to invite us to dinner."

"How you fellers doing?" the big one asks.

"Just great, thanks," Chief says.

"Any luck?"

"Any minute now," Chief says.

"You fellers know they fished this lake out about ten years ago?"

"Oh, yeah, I know that," Chief says. He moves the stick, like he's casting. "Just getting a little practice in."

"Okay. Well, take her easy."

The big one crosses back over the sandbar. He points back at Chief and Hawk to the other big one, who starts chuckling and shaking his head. Chief pulls in his line and casts it a little farther out. The hook snags on something beneath the surface. Pretending he's hooked something, Chief starts pulling, dramatically, gesturing with all his might.

"I think I got something!" Chief says, turning inland. Hawk starts laughing. The big ones start laughing. They all laugh for a moment.

Then they stop laughing.

"You got something!" Hawk yells, staring out at the water.

Chief turns just in time to see a huge striped fish splash into the water, his line dangling from its mouth.

"What do I do?" The stick starts bending out of his hands.

"Set the hook! Set the hook!" Hawk and the big ones yell.

"Set the hook? What's that?"

"Pull!" they yell.

Chief pulls with all his might, straight up in the air. The hook with half the blueberry still attached comes flying toward him, free from the jaws of the great fish, which flickers in the water, as if to wave goodbye.

"You're supposed to pull sideways," Hawk says.

"Oh."

"Say, fellers," a big one yells over. "You fellers hungry?"

"Maybe just a little," Hawk says, springing from the log he's been sitting on.

"'Cause we got us all this here fish, we caught it on the other lake, and we can't eat it all."

"Oh yeah?" Hawk says.

Hawk and Chief sit down on a log across from the big ones. They eat all the leftover fish. Then they eat the leftover instant mashed potatoes, smothered in instant gravy. As darkness falls, a big one drags a log up from the beach and starts a big fire. The big ones offer them a six-day-old tray of coffee cake one of their wives gave them, which they've been hauling around all this time. Hawk and Chief eat the whole tray, stuffing it into their mouths in huge chunks.

"Guess you fellers were a little hungry," a big one says.

"Yes, sir," Chief says. "I guess we were."

"How far you fellers walking to?"

"Portia," Hawk says.

"What, all the way up there?"

Chief sits up. "How far is it?"

Hawk leans back. "Wow," he says. "I could sure go for a smoke right now."

"Not me," a big one says. "Don't smoke."

"Huh. You guys wouldn't have any booze on you, would you?"

"Us? No. We don't drink neither."

"Oh," Hawk says. "Well, I was just wondering."

They all stare at the flames and sparks spiraling into the black sky.

"Well, time we turned in," a big one says. "We're off at the crack of dawn."

"Thank you for the food," Hawk says, getting up slowly and painfully.

"Oh, wait a minute now!" a big one says. "I almost forgot!"

The big one pulls two ice-cold bottles of Coke out of the bottom of one of the coolers and hands them, dripping wet, to Hawk.

"You fellers want these?"

Chief and Hawk return down the beach, sit down on the brittle remains of the cabin's porch, and drink the Cokes, slowly and silently.

*

Morning number six. Chief wakes up to the sound of the big ones' boat buzzing away across the glass lake.

"How much Cheerios we got left?" he asks.

Hawk reaches into his pack and pulls up the bag, empty but for a half-inch of crumbs.

"I dunno," he says. "Maybe two days' worth."

"How many more ramen noodles?"

"Two packs."

"What are we gonna do?"

"Well, I was thinking maybe we could take a day off."

"From hiking?"

"No. From food."

"From food?"

"Yeah. We can fast." Hawk gestures his arms wide out at the lake. Dark clouds circle the far shore, obscuring the tips of a sea of pine trees.

"Fast?"

"We ate good last night. That'll get us through today. We just need to stretch things out a little."

"Stretch things out?"

"Yeah, just, you know, until we find more blueberries. Or until we find somebody else with food."

"Fast?" Chief crawls out of his sleeping bag and starts rolling it up.

"Yeah, you know." Hawk pulls his pack out onto the porch and starts stuffing his gear haphazardly into the main compartment. "We'll tough it out."

With rain sweeping into their faces, they climb up and then down two steep ridges. Chief's heart races as he reaches the tree line, hoping to spot the familiar blue shrubs, but each ridgetop holds only a scattering of blueberry patches, and each branch has been picked clean.

In silence, they stumble forward, ten or fifteen miles. They camp under a ledge, rolling out their bags in dry spots. They boil water and drink it like tea, then fall into dark sleep. In the morning—their seventh—they lick Cheerios crumbs from their fingers, then start again. The trail climbs through tangled roots and boughs. Chief no longer feels hunger, just a hard doughnut hole inside where his stomach was. The nylon hip belt digs stinging red sores into the loose white flesh of what were once his haunches. He falls down a lot now, struggling to keep up with Hawk. His legs slide out on wet roots, and he flops weakly to the ground, then throws himself back up to his feet, red faced and splattered with pine needles and mud.

Another eight miles up trail—hours after they should have had lunch, Chief notes to himself—he catches up with Hawk standing in the mud in a rain-drenched little clearing. Hawk is staring straight down at his feet, a spout of rain pouring off his nose. In the mud, clearly outlined, is a boot print filled with water.

"That's pretty recent," Chief says.

"Huh," Hawk says.

Chief looks around. "Dog prints," he says, pointing up the trail.

"Hmmm," Hawk says.

"So somebody's up ahead of us," Chief says.

"Somebody sure is."

The rain stops, the sun breaks through. They are on a straight path, an elevated old railroad bed. The footing is good, the trail straight and narrow. Straight pine trees, interspersed with white birch trees, pass by on either side as they gain speed. They cover another five miles, another ten, without stopping, the forest streaking by.

Finally, Chief spies a little orange spot on the trail, on the horizon. Panting, Hawk breaks into a jog.

"Easy now," Chief says. "He's still a ways off. Save energy."

Hawk continues to jog. Chief fights to keep up. The orange dot grows into an orange stick, then an orange stick with legs. A little brown dot trots alongside it. As they gain more ground, it becomes the form of a man, limping badly, with a huge pack, and a dog.

"Hey!" Hawk yells. The figure keeps moving.

"Hey!" he yells a little louder. The figure stops, almost stumbling to the ground. Then it turns around.

"Hello!" the man yells.

They catch up with him. He is the most curious-looking person Chief's ever seen—filthy, tall and gangling, a blue bandanna wrapped around his forehead, bent nose, crooked teeth. His backpack is huge. Every conceivable item—pots and pans, socks, tent poles, rope—dangles from various straps. He leans heavily on a crooked branch he has carved into some kind of crutch. His dog, saddled with a huge doggy pack, pants and stares up at Chief curiously.

"Boy, am I glad to see you guys," he says.

"We're glad to see you too," Hawk says.

"I've just been walking alone for days," he says.

"Us too," Chief says.

"I got big blisters," he says.

"That's some pack you've got there," Hawk says, eying the huge frying pan.

"Yeah. Eighty pounds," the man says. "I think I brought too much food."

"What a coincidence," Hawk says. "We just ran out of food."

"Hey, you guys want to have dinner with me? I got plenty of food."

"Oh, really?" Hawk says.

"You guys like falafel?" he says.

"Sure," Hawk says.

"Falafel it is," he says.

Just watching him walk, Chief thinks, is torture. Each step takes him five painful seconds to complete. The next campsite is three miles ahead.

"I'm Tin Pan Tim," he says. "I'm twenty-six-and-a-half years old."

"Is that right?" Hawk says.

"That's my dog there, Ole Yeller," Tin Pan Tim says.

"Oh yeah?" Chief says. "Like the TV show?"

"No!" Tin Pan Tim yells. "I never heard of any TV show called Ole Yeller! Never! I made the name up myself. Because he's yeller."

"Oh."

"Ole Yeller is the most loyal dog ever. He follows me everywhere. He pulled me out of a lake once when I was drowning. Once two guys were hassling me, and he went to the police station and barked 'til they came and got the guys."

"Really," Chief says.

"You need a hand with that backpack, Tin Pan Tim?" Hawk asks. "That way, we can move along a little quicker. You know, because it's getting dark."

"Sure!"

Hawk and Chief each take a strap. The backpack is incredibly heavy.

A lake appears through the woods. They lead Tin Pan Tim and Ole Yeller through the forest, away from the trail, pushing their way through huge ferns. They break out onto a beautiful beach on another beautiful lake. Huge sand-washed logs lay on top of smooth sand. Hawk and Chief set up their tent on one side of a large log; Tin Pan Tim sets his up on the other.

Ole Yeller sits down next to Chief. Tin Pan Tim, still setting up his tent, yells, "Here, boy!" Ole Yeller looks at him, then back at Chief. She wags her tail.

"I said, 'Here, boy!'"

Ole Yeller doesn't budge. Suddenly Tin Pan Tim gets up, takes him by the collar, and drags him over to his tent site. Ole Yeller lies in the sand, looking at Chief forlornly.

"You quit staring at him!" Tin Pan Tim yells. "You're my dog! You're not his darn dog!" He starts his camp stove, then rolls twelve little balls of dough with his dirty hands. He pulls out a huge canister of cooking oil, fills the pan, and starts cooking.

"This should just take a minute," he says. "Just enough time to work on my feet."

Hawk stares at the balls of breaded chickpea, shrinking and browning in the pan. Chief watches Tin Pan Tim tug off his boots, then socks. Dozens of little Band-Aids cover his toes, his ankles, the bottoms of his feet, and his heels. He peels them off, one by one, exposing huge red holes in his feet. Then he takes out a quart container of Morton's salt.

"That's a lot of salt," Hawk says.

"You can never have too much salt," Tin Pan Tim says. He pours a handful of salt into his hand. Then he pours it straight into a gaping pink hole on his heel.

"*Eeeeee!*" Tin Pan Tim's screams echo off the far side of the lake. Ole Yeller howls and runs toward Chief, who pushes him back toward Tin Pan Tim.

"They say salt's good for blisters," Tin Pan Tim says, grimacing, preparing to pour more into the next blister. "They say it makes them feel better. They better feel better cuz we got a long ways to go, don't we, Ole Yeller? We're going all the way out to Grizzletown, way upland."

The sun is setting in oranges and reds over the lake. Tin Pan Tim slowly turns the falafel balls over, again and again, in the pan full of oil. They grow brown and shrivel. After an hour of Tin Pan Tim alternately turning the falafels, salting his blisters, and howling, he finally takes the little balls out of the pan.

"Here's four for you," he says to Chief, "and here's three for you," he says to Hawk.

Tiny and tasteless, they are wolfed down in three fast bites.

Chief wakes up to the smell of pancakes.

Tin Pan Tim sits in front of his tent, eating the last few bites of a huge stack of pancakes, buried in syrup. Ole Yeller licks the last strands of batter from a bowl.

"Pancakes, huh," Hawk says.

Tin Pan Tim says nothing. Wrapped up in bandages, his feet look a whole lot worse. He hobbles around his campsite, moving pots and pans and clothing and food containers into assorted stacks, but doesn't appear to be packing them.

After a few minutes trying to make small talk, Hawk shrugs to Chief. They pack up their tent and bags and get ready to head out.

"You guys aren't just leaving me here, are you?" Tin Pan Tim asks.

"Well, we sorta gotta get moving," Chief says. "You know. Gotta push on to Portia."

"Take me with you!" Tin Pan Tim pleads. "We'll walk a ways, and I'll make you guys lunch! I'll make a big lunch! We'll have hummus sandwiches with cheese. I got tahini sauce. I'll grill them up. What do you say?"

"Well, okay," Hawk says, taking his pack off.

They help Tin Pan Tim get his tent down and get the doggy pack strapped onto Ole Yeller. Chief flinches watching Tin Pan Tim get his socks and boots back on, then try to pull the huge backpack back on. By late morning they are back on the trail.

Hollow, Chief tries not to fixate on what the containers of food may hold. He tries to cover some distance. Ole Yeller follows Chief and Hawk, and the distance quickly grows between the three of them and Tin Pan Tim. The forest wraps itself around them; it has no smell or temperature. At each bend in the trail, Tin Pan Tim disappears for a minute or two, then yells, "Wait up!" This goes on for a few hours.

"It's got to be lunchtime by now," Hawk says at one point when they are ahead a few steps.

"This isn't going to work," Chief says. "At this pace, we're only going to make it five miles a day. We got forty miles left to go."

"I wonder how tahini sauce keeps after a week in a backpack?" Hawk says.

"Wait up!" Tin Pan Tim yells again from the woods behind them.

Suddenly the trail emerges onto what looks like a wooden dock, jutting out into a new lake. A seaplane is tied up at the end of the dock. Two men stand looking at them.

"How you doing?" Chief asks.

"Not so bad," one of the men says. He's holding a beer. "Lost, maybe a little."

"We saw this dock here and landed," the other says. "But it don't seem to be attached to nothing."

"Where did you come up from?"

"Down around Portia, I think."

Tin Pan Tim bursts out of the woods.

"You guys headed back to Portia?" he asks.

"Yeah."

"Can I bum a ride in the back of your plane? Me and my dog?"

"Sure."

Suddenly filled with energy, Tin Pan Tim runs down the dock and throws his huge pack into the back of the plane, climbs in, and beckons Ole Yeller. The dog looks at Chief longingly, then puts his head down and climbs in.

"I thought you were walking all the way to Grizzletown?" Chief says.

"Changed my mind," Tin Pan Tim says.

"So then you won't be needing all that food," Hawk says. But the plane lurches away from the dock as he says it.

"See ya!" Tin Pan Tim yells, waving from the little window. He looks happy for the first time since they met him, Chief has to admit. The plane turns a corner and disappears.

"I really could have gone for that hummus sandwich," Hawk says.

The trail's white blazes become blinking lights, leading them deeper into the forest. It doesn't matter any more if it's getting dark or if it's still daylight. Chief follows Hawk's bent frame, the half-empty pack bobbing ahead in the woods. He can't remember if he's slept or if it's day eight or nine. He can't remember if Tin Pan Tim really happened or if it was all a dream. He keeps imagining Ole Yeller panting next to him, but when he turns, the dog is not there. The pain in his legs has turned to numbness; the sharp branches that claw at him no longer matter.

There's a moment when the trail works its way up onto an open ledge. Between some of the rocks are blueberry bushes, but they've been picked over by bears or birds. Only a few remain, which Chief and Hawk search for crazily, even though they're wrinkled and sour.

The trail pitches back down into a grove of pine trees, then crosses something like a dirt road before scaling a steeper ledge. Chief finds Hawk lying face down in the dirt. He kicks the sole of Hawk's boot.

"We gotta keep moving," Chief says. "If we stop, we're going to die out here."

"I'm really sorry, man."

"Sorry? Why are you sorry?"

"I'm full of shit, man," Hawk whispers into the ground. "Can I let you in on a little secret? I never been on this here particular part of the trail before. I sort of don't know what I'm doing out here. We might be a little bit lost."

"Yeah," Chief says. "I was sort of starting to figure that out."

"Sorry, man."

Chief watches his hand fit itself around a rock; it fits into his hand perfectly. He watches with a sort of delirious fascination as his arm lifts the rock and swings down, cracking into Hawk's head.

"Hey, man," Chief whispers. "I'm sorry too."

It's late afternoon. Chief finds himself on high, serrated ledges, enveloped in cloud and fog, unprotected. A cold, misty rain penetrates his seams. Then he crashes madly down a steep, soft trail, arms flopping wildly at his sides. In a small clearing at the bottom, a late sun bursts through. The forest before him is impenetrable. He's lost track of the trail and the blazes. Chief lies down on the wet grass, surrounded by tiny flowers, and stares up at purple stains of clouds.

"Sherbet," he mumbles. "Rainbow sherbet, please."

He starts floating, slowly, his whole body rising just above the treetops, the pine branches gently brushing him homeward. His eyes close, then open. It's still light out. Above him, framed by trees, is the perfectly round, freckled, blushing face of a girl, maybe just a teenager, in a blue print dress. Her arms, burnt red at the tops, are like huge loaves of Wonder Bread. Chief sits up to look at her.

"Are you all right, sir?"

"Am I dead?"

She giggles deep within herself, like the rustling of pebbles. "You must be hungry, you poor fellow. You look so hungry. Are you hungry?" She pulls open a wicker picnic basket, reaches in, and pulls out a sandwich.

"Yes. I think I am hungry."

"Would you like a ham sandwich?"

"A ham sandwich would be nice."

He eats the huge ham sandwich, with relish and American cheese, in four bites. She crouches next to him, smiling.

"Thank you," he says.

She reaches into the basket again.

"Say, would you like a cream pie?"

"That sounds great," Chief says, pulling a round black cake with white cream filling out of the wax paper. He eats it in two bites. "Thank you again."

"Well, you're very welcome."

Chief looks around the clearing and into the dark forest that surrounds them. "But where did you come from?"

"From Portia. My daddy owns a cannery. He brought us up here to have a picnic. I guess I made too much food."

"Well, I'm glad you made too much food."

"There's plenty more here," she says, reaching into her basket again. "Would you like a turkey sandwich? Would you like a chicken salad sandwich? Another cream pie? There's about four more, I guess."

"Thanks." Chief takes everything and piles it on his pack.

Someone shouts from deep within the woods.

"Well, I guess I better get going," she says. "That's my dad." She brushes the front of her dress off, gets up, and waves briefly.

"Hey," Chief says. She stops and turns.

"Yes?"

"Do you know how much farther it is to Portia?"

"But that's where you are." She waves one of her huge, bare arms toward the path. "Just a ways down this dirt path. Just over that hill."

"Thank you." Chief watches her slowly disappear into the woods, a shrinking blue circle dissipating into a larger black one. He carefully packs most of the food into his backpack.

He eats two more cream pies, steadily and carefully, as a chocolate darkness pours itself into the woods all around him.

FROM *THE ONLY PLANET GUIDE:* GETTING THERE AND GETTING AROUND

As frustrating as it may seem, travel to and around the Grizzle Peninsula brings out the pioneer spirit in everyone who makes it that far. The journey cannot fail to remind all who attempt it of the time-honored traveler's creed that "Getting there is half the fun." There are three ways to get to the Grizzle Peninsula: by airplane, ferry, or motor vehicle.

Air travel: Flying to Petrolia, the region's metropolis (a sad place, formerly built as military housing, now consisting of motels, fast-food restaurants, and seedy bars), can be an adventure in itself. Several commercial airlines now fly round trip into Petrolia. Once there, better-resourced visitors can quickly (but expensively) rent a car to get around. Many backpackers who can afford to do so take this route for easy access to adventures in the Great Gulf Wilderness, just an eight-hour drive southwest. There are legends of unconventional travel methods involving bootleggers who fly small, lightweight aircraft called "skeeters" around the peninsula, carrying people and supplies to and from the settlements, working through the occupation, and eluding military radar due to their wood-and-canvas structure. The author strongly advises against getting in an unregistered plane with anybody; many of the disappearances rumored to occur each year are believed to happen in unregistered flights.

Ferry service: Ferries run up the coast during the summer months, arriving in the small West Coast town of Portia at the southern end of the peninsula. Many travelers come by ferry and intend to hitchhike up the peninsula from Portia. However, it is estimated that more than 80 percent of the summer travelers to the Grizzle Peninsula never make it out of Portia. Many of the backpackers and travelers who make the long trip by ferry, with thoughts of exploring inland, struggle to find the impetus to push further once they see the dark, forbidding forests and jagged snow-capped peaks stretching endlessly into the horizon. If this happens to you on your first trip to Grizzle, you are not alone. Portia and its surroundings offer more than enough adventure and excitement for its visitors (see "Portia and its Surroundings," below).

Car travel: The third way, by car, takes drivers up over a pass on the eastern coast via the Old Soldier's Highway, winds down to Portia, and then twists and turns its way up through the wilds of the peninsula, petering out just beyond Petrolia. The road has yet to be paved (and if the environmentalists have it their way, it never will be) beyond Portia. The Old Soldier's Highway has been called "the automobile graveyard;" it has been the end of many a car without the axle strength and undercarriage to survive this notorious gravel road, as demonstrated by dozens of abandoned vehicles rusting on its sides. Many RV camper enthusiasts drive only as far as Portia before loading onto the ferry for the trip home.

A note about the Old Soldier's Highway: The Old Soldier's Highway was originally carved out of the peninsula's forests, granite and mud during the Great Panic of 1942, when invasion from foreign entities seemed all but certain. Previously, the peninsula was occupied by only a small handful of coastal fishing villages; rarely did even its year-round residents venture into its interior. The Great Panic *sent a wave of some five thousand ill-trained, ill-suited soldiers up from tropical bases; they found themselves fighting their own war of survival in the frozen, barren wilderness, carving a road from Portia to Petrolia to create a forward base (see History). It is believed that many convict teams became lost in the wilderness or escaped: many years later, traces of mysterious hand-cut paths are still discovered, twisting through the mountains from Portia to the Great Gulf and possibly beyond.*

JUNE 1983

Ernie on the
Old Soldier's Highway

A cold mist blows over the tops of the pine trees. It coats Ernie's anorak and soaks his boots. He stands shaking for an hour. A Winnebago passes. It pulls over and stops on the shoulder. Pink lace curtains flap from a tiny rear window. They must be lost, Ernie figures.

The camper honks. A fleshy, sleeveless arm waves to him from the cab.

"This here the road to Portia?" the driver calls to him.

"Yeah," Ernie says.

"Well, get in!" she yells. "We're not going to bite you!"

A side door swings open. Ernie climbs in and sits in a plush velvet chair. He's surrounded by beige and brown carpet and paneling, cabinets and drawers. He glances over his shoulder. A low toilet peeks from behind a very small door. Two elderly women smile at him from the front seats. A huge plastic cruci-fix hangs from the rearview mirror. The smell of perfume over-whelms him.

"You look like you need a nice glass of iced tea," the pas-senger says. She gets up and waddles past him to the tiny kitchenette.

"Yes, sir," the driver says. She turns the camper back out onto the highway. "You sure look like you've been out here a while." Ernie leans back in his soft armchair.

Gripping the counter with one hand, the elderly passenger hands him an iced tea, then a paper plate filled with Oreo cookies. "No fancy china, sorry," she says, then pulls herself back up into her seat.

"I'm Rosemarie. Corinne here is my copilot," the driver says. She brushes back a mane of white hair. She holds a camcorder in her lap with one hand; the other pins a dog-eared book, a road atlas, against the steering wheel. She cranes her neck to squint at maps she's ripped out of the book and taped to the ceiling. "How far are you going?" she asks.

"Portia," he says. "I'm meeting a friend there."

"Well," Rosemarie says, flipping through the Milepost. "We're going toward Portia, but a little slow. If you want to jump out and see if you can find a faster ride, you just let us know."

"How about some homemade popcorn?" Corinne asks. "Or I can make some nachos, if you like them. You like nachos?"

Ernie looks out through the lace curtains. The forest rolls slowly by.

"Oh, yes," he says. "Nachos would be great."

Hours pass. The sky darkens. Sheets of cold rain sweep against the windshield. Outside, the soaked tundra shimmers, silver and green, punctuated by angry dead trees. Rosemarie turns up the heat. She tells Ernie about the little town they're from, the church where they run the youth program, the axle they broke on the way.

"When that axle broke, we had half a mind just to turn around right there, didn't we, Corinne?"

"Oh, yes," Corinne says.

"But like I said, imagine what the pioneers would have done. Would they have turned around and gone home?"

"No, sir."

"It's like I always say, when life gives you lemons..."

"You make lemonade," Corinne says quickly.

Rosemarie takes a long look at Ernie through the rearview mirror. Ernie stops trying to stuff strands of oily hair up under his baseball cap. He scratches the thick stubble on his neck. He looks down at his hands; his nails are black. When he looks up again, Rosemarie's eyes are back on the road.

"Are you going to be roughnecking up here?" she asks.

"What's that?"

"She wants to know if you've got work on the pipelines," Corinne says.

"Who, me? No."

"Fishing boat?"

"No, nothing like that."

"Canneries? You going to work the canneries?"

"I don't know." Ernie starts scratching again, this time all over. "I'm going to get work as soon as I hook up with my friend. She's coming up to meet me on the ferry."

"That's some drive," Rosemarie says.

"I think we can still get work, I think, up the coast. We're thinking of maybe going all the way out to Grizzletown."

"Supposed to be really something out there."

"Yeah, it's really beautiful," Ernie says. He brushes salt off his drying anorak. It leaves white flecks on the upholstery. "At least I hear it is. I hear there's lots of work out there, this time of year. Canneries, fishing boats. I hear they're always looking for people, and they pay ten bucks an hour. But it's way out on the coast in the backcountry. You gotta walk there, I guess."

The snacks keep coming: corn chips and pretzels and soda. Ernie starts dozing. He half-dreams, half-remembers calling Eva from the pay phone, only in the dream he's together, standing erect. His voice is low, confident. Everything's okay now. He's got a plan. She's coming for sure.

Ernie wakes up to an oncoming horn. Rosemarie pulls the camper back into her lane.

"Do you know how they built this highway?" Ernie says, fighting to wake up.

"I can't imagine," Rosemarie says. She rubs her eyes and squints at the maps. Corinne snores by her side.

"I'm reading a book about it. It was the beginning of the Great Panic. The enemy took a couple of islands on the coast, so we built this highway. So we could ship supplies up. So we could counterattack. In the islands."

"You don't say."

"Yeah. But it was a division of convicts from way downland. They had to build the highway. They got stuck out here in little canvas tents. Freezing cold. They worked through the winter. All hand tools. They built bridges, cut embankments. They finished a year ahead of schedule. But a bunch of them disappeared in the woods or froze to death doing it."

"Well now, ain't that something."

"What's that?" Corinne asks suddenly.

"Ernie's telling us about a book he's reading, about the convicts who built this here highway."

"The what?"

"The convicts!" Rosemarie yells. "They built the highway!"

A town appears suddenly—first cabins, then little houses, then stores. Rosemarie drives the camper past a strip of one-story buildings. Ernie peers through the curtains at glowing beer signs in windows: Labatt, Molson, Anchor Steam, Budweiser. Rosemarie pulls into a gas station. A large wood-carved lumberjack waves from the porch. Taped to his axe is a sign: "12-pack $8.99."

"This is the place!" she yells. "We fill the tank, they let us camp out back for free!" Rosemarie climbs down from the driver's seat and enters the store, leaving Ernie and Corinne alone in the camper.

"Ain't she something," Corinne says.

"Yes, she is," Ernie says.

"Her chiropractor told her don't do it. Said she couldn't take it. She broke her neck, you see. Four summers ago. In the accident. Broke her dang neck."

"Wow," Ernie says. "She's lucky."

"Hardly," Corinne says. "She's hardly that."

"Oh."

"The Lord giveth, and the Lord taketh away. It's not for us to question why."

Rosemarie reappears. She's smiling. "Good news!" she says as she pulls herself up into the driver's seat. "There's room out back, one more spot for a camper. And the man says you can set up your tent right back behind there. You have a tent in that backpack of yours, don't you?"

Ernie peers out at a sea of industrial waste scattered under the trees. "Yeah."

"Well, we turn in early. We're just a couple of old ladies. I guess we'll see you in the morning. Do you want to ride with us tomorrow?"

"Yeah, that would be great," Ernie says. "Thanks." He grabs his backpack and climbs down, closing the screen door behind him.

Ernie wakes up to the wild buzz of camper generators. He lies in the tent for a while, trying to remember what he told Eva. It was two weeks ago. He was pretty hammered. He thinks he convinced her he was sober. She was pretty sure she was coming up. He remembers telling her he has jobs lined up, places to stay. In the fall they could work their way back down land, follow the coast. Maybe get home by Christmas.

Ernie climbs out of his tent, set up between two rusting, abandoned meat freezers. He gathers his beer cans and tucks them behind one of the freezers. Rosemarie's camper sits nearby, the lace curtains drawn shut. He walks to the general store, buys a cup of coffee, and returns to his tent site. He perches on top of one of the freezers and re-enters his book. While the convicts fight through the winter to finish the highway, a team of pilots stationed on a makeshift airbase on the islands make raids on the enemy positions. The weather's terrible, their weaponry is outdated, and they have few supplies. The isolation starts to get to the pilots. They turn violent, murder each other, have nervous breakdowns. They fight over the privilege of flying suicide missions.

Ernie gets up for another cup of coffee. Halfway across the parking lot he hears, "Hey! Hey, you!" He turns to face a creased old man, grinning in his pajamas.

"You, now, son, you want some coffee? C'mere with me. I'll get you some coffee."

He waves Ernie toward his camper, a smaller model than Rosemarie's. "C'mon now, I won't bite you. You just come on over here."

Ernie follows him into the compact vehicle. He fits himself into a tiny kitchen booth across from the man. A red-haired woman in a nightgown squints through huge glasses. She puts down a pot of coffee. The old man fills Ernie's cup, then his own.

"That's my wife, Barbara," the man says. "I'm Eugene."

Ernie takes a sip and winces. "Wow," he says. "That's some coffee."

"We drove ourselves all the way up here," Eugene says.

"That's a long ways," Ernie says.

"Drove all the way up, far as we could. Drove all the way up to see that big old pipeline, up where the road ends."

"That must have been something," Ernie says.

"That ain't nothing," Eugene says. "Nothing but a load of crap. Them goddamn oil companies think they got it all figured out. They don't know nothing."

"You want some more coffee, hon?" Barbara asks Ernie.

"My old man worked twenty years for the refinery up there outside Petrolia. Didn't have no pipeline then. Twenty years, never missed a day sick. One day a jack came down, smashed his hand flat. They let him go that day. No pension. Nothing."

Somebody bangs on the screen door.

"That's my hitchhiker," Rosemarie calls to Barbara. "You can't have him." Barbara laughs.

"Well, if you're ever in our neighborhood," Eugene says, "be sure to stop on by. We're in the trailer parked behind the Bible Baptist Church."

Rosemarie twists her head around to squint at the new map she's taped to the ceiling.

"Portia Junction," Rosemarie says. "Here we come."

"Almost Portia," Ernie says. His head is throbbing.

"Now, did you say you're going to Portia or Portia Junction?" Corinne asks.

"I'm going to Portia," Ernie says. "I think. I'm meeting her in Portia."

"Now I would have sworn you said Portia Junction," Corinne says.

"Portia, Portia Junction," Rosemarie says. "Can't be much distance from one to another. Do you need more air conditioning back there? Do you need me to turn up the air conditioner?"

"No, thanks."

"Maybe you need a drink," Corinne says, not turning. "Like some water."

"I'm okay, thanks."

"You know now, if we're going too slow for you, you can get another ride. If you have to get to where you're going in a hurry."

"Thanks," he says.

"Would you like some chips? Is it too early?"

"No, not at all, thanks. I'm grateful for the ride."

Corinne is silent, staring ahead at the long caravan of Winnebagos.

"Because we sure enjoy the company," Rosemarie continues. "It sure is nice of you to keep a couple of old ladies company."

"Chips would be great, thanks," Ernie says. "Never too early for chips."

In the middle of a treeless wilderness, signs and flags mark the sudden approach of a marshal checkpoint. Rosemarie starts rubbing her neck.

"Now this should only take a minute," she says.

"Unless, of course, someone's carrying drugs," Corinne adds.

"Hello," the marshal says as they pull up.

"Just a couple of old ladies out for a drive, marshal!" Rosemarie says. The marshal climbs up to Rosemarie's window and peers at Ernie's backpack, then directly at Ernie.

"You folks all got a driver's license?" the marshal asks. His voice is deep, but his face is young, covered in red freckles.

"Hand him your driver's license, Ernie."

"I've got a passport."

The marshal glances at the pack again. "No driver's license?"

"I don't drive."

"Huh," Corinne says, staring straight ahead.

"You don't drive?" the marshal asks. "You've never driven?"

"No," Ernie says, scratching. "I'm a lousy driver."

"How do you know if you've never driven?"

Ernie shrugs. Rosemarie and Corinne tuck their licenses back into their handbags.

"Well, we're looking for a bad guy, but I guess you ain't him." The marshal glances at the passport and hands it back to Ernie. "You have a great trip," he says to Rosemarie.

They drive along a winding river. Dark clouds cling to the top of stark mountains. At six o'clock, Rosemarie pulls over next to a beautiful glacial lake shining through the windshield.

"Let's stop for dinner, gang," she says. "We can push on to Portia Junction after dinner. This spot here's just a little too perfect not to have dinner."

Corinne silently prepares a tuna casserole, potato chips, and orange soda. She hasn't spoken all day. Ernie stares out at the lake, then jumps up to help unfold the little dining table. Moving much more slowly, Rosemarie reaches into a drawer for forks and knives.

"Let me help you set the table," Ernie says.

"No, sir. You're our guest here," she says, swiveling her head from side to side and grimacing. "Be it ever so humble." They sit down around the table. Corinne and Rosemarie hold hands and reach for Ernie's. Their hands are clean and weight-less. Ernie realizes how grimy he must feel, how bad he must smell. They don't seem to notice. Rosemarie takes a deep breath.

"Dear Lord," she begins, "we thank you for this wonderful day and for seeing us through another day's journey in safety. We thank you for helping me with my neck, for keeping it from going out again. We thank you for keeping Corinne's bum leg from swelling up. Thank you, Lord, for keeping the generator running. Thank you for the new axle, which is just humming right along. We thank you for the road conditions, much better, I'd say, than yesterday, but nobody's complaining about yesterday. And dear Lord, I'm sorry and I'm praying for that squirrel I pegged. Lord, I thank you for taking Marty back into your heart and for sending him once to me, to enrich my life. And dear Lord…"

She grips Ernie's sweat-soaked hand a little harder.

"…we thank you, last and not least, for bringing this young man into our lives and for the friendship and comfort he's providing to us, and we hope too that you help us to help him find his way to Portia Junction or Portia. And dear Lord, we hope you help him find his friend, and himself, and a purpose for this journey he's on."

"Amen," Corinne says.

Ernie bites into a spoonful of casserole. "Was Marty your husband?" he asks.

"Marty was my boy," Rosemarie answers.

They chew in silence for a while.

"She must be very brave," Rosemarie says.

"Who's that?"

"Your friend you're meeting. Coming up here, all that way, by herself. That's some long journey for a young lady, all by herself. She must be very brave."

"Yeah."

"Here." Rosemarie smiles, passing a plastic red bowl. "Have some more chips."

In the middle of Portia Junction, there's a huge signboard with mileage signs and arrows pointing to every possible destination: Portia, Petrolia, Can-Town, Great Gulf Wilderness Regional Park. The light fades behind distant blue mountains. They stare up at all the signs.

"So is it Portia or Portia Junction?" Rosemarie asks Ernie. She's holding her head with both hands and wincing.

"It's Portia, I think," Ernie says, staring at the signpost for Portia. "I think I said I would meet her in Portia."

"Well, we're going to drive down a little farther tonight toward Portia. We're just going to camp on the side of the road.

We'll find a good spot where you can pitch your tent. Then in the morning, we'll make sure to get you to Portia to meet your friend."

Rosemarie pulls over in a gravel turnoff boxed in by huge granite peaks. Ernie climbs up a little hill, just out of sight of the camper, and pitches his tent. He rolls out his sleeping bag and lies down to read a chapter of the book in the fading light. Supplied by land from the highway, the soldiers mount their first amphibious assault of the war against the soldiers on the island. The landing craft crashes into coral reefs a thousand feet from shore, drowning hundreds of men. The first soldiers to make the beach are run over by their own tanks. The men fight through snow and rain, inch by inch, to take the island. A hundred have their feet amputated for frostbite. The last group of enemy soldiers makes a surprise bayonet charge into the field hospital. They kill a dozen amputees, then pull grenades out and blow themselves up. It's too dark to read any more. Ernie lies still in the tent. The highway builders spin in his head, visible breath blowing from their nostrils, driving pickaxes into ice and dirt. The pilots, the soldiers who built the highway, the soldiers who fought on the island, Eugene's dad. They had to come up here, he thinks. They did what they had to do.

He hears a lone car pass somewhere out in the woods, on the distant highway, the road to Portia. What if it's Eva? What if she's driving back and forth between Portia and Portia Junction looking for him? What if they came this close and couldn't find each other? A shiver passes through him. Eva's not going to be there, he thinks. She didn't sound convinced at all. She always knew when he was drunk. She wasn't going to drive two thousand miles up here for him.

It's the first night Ernie's been without a drink since the canyon with Eva. The screams of strange insects and birds fill the woods. He starts twitching—first his hands and feet, then his entire body.

"Ernie!" he hears from the woods.

With a flashlight, Ernie finds his way back down to the camper. Corinne's silhouette stands at the screen door. She's in her nightgown and robe, her hair in curlers, rubbing her knee with her hand.

"It's Rosemarie," Corinne says. "She needs you."

Ernie climbs in. Rosemarie sits perfectly still in the armchair Ernie's occupied for the past few days. Her eyes are closed, and she's barefoot in a long white gown.

"I need you to do something for me," Rosemarie says. Her eyelids flutter. She presses them shut. "Can you do something for me?"

"Sure, Rosemarie. What do you need me to do?"

"I need you to set my neck. I'll show you how. Can you do it?"

Ernie looks over at Corinne, who retreats to her passenger seat, ringing her hands.

"I'm not strong enough," Corinne whispers. "I tried. I just can't."

"I need you to come stand behind me," Rosemarie says. Ernie obeys. "Now I need you to put your arm around my head, like so." She guides his right hand to hold her in a gentle headlock position. Her chin rests inside his elbow. Her hands hold tightly to his forearm.

"Now I need you to place your other hand against the base of my skull, like this." She guides Ernie's shaking left hand to the back of her head, against the smooth ripples of her hair.

"Now I need you to jerk my head up, real hard, as hard and as fast as you can."

"I can't do that," Ernie says.

"You can. Yes, you can. You have to."

Ernie takes a deep breath. Still shuddering, he feels a sudden surge. He snaps Rosemarie's head up as hard as he can. There's a loud crack, then a crunching sound. He releases her. He's sure that he broke her neck. Rosemarie sits still for a moment, then runs a hand up to reposition her hair on her shoulders. She rolls her neck around like she's just woken from a long nap. She beams up at Ernie.

"That will do it, Ernie. God bless you, and good night."

Her smell is all around him now. She smells so sweet, Ernie thinks. Like flowers.

JULY 1983

FROM *THE ONLY PLANET GUIDE*: PORTIA AND SURROUNDINGS

After a two-week hitchhike, or after a four-day ferry trip up the coast, entering the fishing village of Portia's harbor as the sun sets can be an intoxicating experience. After days of passing through the mountains by car or ferry, then through the narrows—wooded, formless islands along the coastline— a sudden string of yellow lights, glowing along a tangle of piers strung out on a sandbar, announce your arrival. A cruise ship or two may be in port, and huge tankers and barges lurch in and out of the narrows; scores of commercial fishing boats and floating canneries dodge between them. Eagles circle above. Behind the town, coastal mountains wind up to snow-capped peaks; a glacier spills its weird blue light into the water just up the coast.

Stepping off the ferry, you will realize before long that first impressions can be deceiving and the sense of intoxica- tion all too literal. Portia—"The Gateway to the Last Great Wilderness," as banners hanging over Main Street pro- claim—is a boomtown that has not kept pace with the boom. This is in part due to its physical location on a narrow tangle of land caught between towering mountains and the ocean. The opening of the fisheries has brought a great industry that must share this narrow plot with everything that is shipped upland into the Grizzle Interior from this spot. The sensation for the traveler is that you are trapped in a funnel and some- how must squeeze your way through. Portia's few streets are lined with bars and saloons where hundreds of backpackers elbow up next to fishermen, cruise ship tourists, and snake-

oil salesmen trying to get you to buy them the next round. Portia is a place of great beauty and of great despair; whether you've approached by ferry, by car, or by foot via the Old Soldier's Highway, it's best to finish your beer quickly and move in for the interior.

Places to stay: *For those expecting to find clean sheets and a comfy pillow after their long journey, Portia offers very little in the way of amenities. For the budget traveler, the best bargain is Portia Municipal Campground, located two miles up the winding Portage Road. The campground costs $10 per campsite per night (showers are free). It features 120 campsites, winding in loops through dense forest. In July and August, up to one hundred of these sites may be occupied by large campers and trailers; those who pitch tents may find themselves surrounded by the sounds of diesel generators and televisions. For people with money to burn, a few small inns on Main Street offer private rooms and baths. The best of these options may be Joe's Portage Parlor ($50 per night), located above Joe's Hunter and Trapper Outlet at 52 Main Street. (If you are lucky enough to meet Joe, don't ask him how he lost his right thumb.) For those ready to really rough it, numerous off-the-map campsites pop up in the forests surrounding Portia, housing hundreds of vagabonds in makeshift tents and huts; select these communities at your own risk.*

Things to do: *After you've settled in, you can experience local flavor at several local watering holes, most notably the Foggy Bottom. With pool tables and occasional live music, the Foggy Bottom attracts a range of crowds; some nights it is filled with fishermen, other nights with cruise ship tourists. During the day, hiking in this region is spectacular, especially east along the Coastal Trail and in the Portage Preserve, the mountains all car travelers must pass through on their way inland, up the peninsula, or back toward the mainland (free maps available at the campground office).*

Ernie in the campground

When Ernie wakes up, he puts his hand against the edge of the tent. It's dry! He crawls out under the fly, dragging his sleeping bag behind him. This is the state campground, he remembers; he's been here three days. It is the same, but it is different.

Sunlight pours down between the massive old piney branches through the rich canopy above him; things that have been brown and black for the past week are now bright red and green and orange. The top of the picnic table is dry. It's dry! He spreads the sleeping bag out across the table in the little patch of sunlight, and he sits down on the dry end of the bench. He thinks of other things he needs to pull out and dry off—clothes, boots—but he sits in the sunlight, letting the warmth sink into his bones. The forest around him smells like somebody blew up a pinecone. He sits there for some time. He thinks about starting the stove and getting some instant coffee going, but that involves walking to the campsite spigot to get water. The spigot is next to the ranger station, and he is considering ducking the ranger, having not paid yet for the prior night and not wanting to pay for the next. Ernie isn't out of money yet, but he keeps thinking if he slips out of the campground and keeps the twenty or thirty bucks, he'll be better off.

Ernie sits there, thinking about how much instant coffee he has left when—slap—a screen door slams in the woods just behind his tent. He looks over the back of his tent. A huge, wood-paneled bus—like a hobbit house on wheels, really—is parked in the next campsite. Standing in front of it, in another half-beam of morning sunlight, are three little children—maybe six, maybe four, and maybe two—of undeterminable sex. They have mountains of long yellow hair that covers their faces like blankets. They are shirtless, all wearing pajama bottoms, except for the littlest, who is naked and is peeing onto the rain fly of Ernie's tent. All three stare at Ernie, not with excitement or interest, but like he is a tyrannosaurus passing a little pack of triceratops—don't mess with me, their sparkling little triceratops eyes seem to say, and I won't mess with you.

"You're peeing on my tent," Ernie says to the youngest.

After a few seconds, Ernie turns to the oldest.

"Do you think you can get her to stop peeing on my tent?"

"*His* name is Blue," the oldest says. "And he needs to pee outside, not in our house. This is what the father has taught us."

As this one speaks, a fourth, then a fifth child, maybe three and five, climb down a ladder on the side of the bus/hobbit house.

"Are you all going to pee on my tent?" Ernie asks.

"No," the spokesperson says. "We are not going to pee on your tent."

Three more children climb out of another porthole. They all stand in line, holding themselves, waiting to pee on the side of Ernie's tent. Someone, an adult male, starts banging pans inside the thing, then yells a string of obscenities, then bangs more pans.

"That is the father," the spokesperson says. "It appears he is awake."

"The father is fixing the sink," another one, a porthole-dweller, says. "He can fix anything. He built our house."

The spokesperson waves a naked arm at the squeaking, rocking vehicle.

"People call it a bus because it has wheels, but the father tells us that wheels only connect us to the earth."

One of the little ones, after peeing, climbs into Ernie's lap and examines his/her dirt-caked toes. Others sit around him at the picnic table, folding their arms and staring at him. A large pot whistles out of one of the portholes and crashes against the adjacent firepit; another torrent of cursing follows.

"This is our home now," the spokesperson states. "This is where we live."

"That's terrific," Ernie says. "Listen, I've got to go someplace. Why don't you guys go eat breakfast? Why don't you go pee somewhere else?" He lifts the child from his lap and puts him or her down on the bench; the child stares up at him curiously. Ernie starts walking to the ranger station. He turns around; the children are unzipping his tent. Oh, Lord. Are they going to crap in there? But then more cursing bellows from the hobbit bus. The children all retreat into the woods and back to the bus.

The sky darkens, the temperature plummets, and it starts raining again. Ernie wraps his poncho around his shoulders. A gentle pat of rain on the road, the trees, the Winnebagos becomes a roar that drowns out all the other sounds. Ernie remembers now that he woke up in the middle of the night to the sound of a lone gunshot somewhere in the woods. As he walks toward the ranger station, he considers asking about it. When he enters, he's met with steaming, droopy air hissing from a little space heater. The screen door slams behind him. The tall, young ranger, the same kid who's been here every morning, looks up from a pile of forms and shakes his head, a shaggy mane of blond hair stuffed under a ranger cap.

"'Nother night?"

"Yup."

"Site fifty-nine. Right?"

"Yup." Ernie fills out the form, pulls damp, crumpled bills from his pocket, and counts out ten ones.

"Sure adds up, doesn't it."

"Yup."

"Hey," the ranger whispers, although no one else is there. "You know there's a free campsite, right? They call it the secret campsite."

"Really?"

"Yeah, there's a little encampment. A lot of seasonal workers live there 'cause it's free. It's about a mile in the woods. There's a little trail behind the shower building. There's a guy who seems to be in charge, I guess. He's there all the time. They call him Chief. I guess you ask him if it's okay to stay there. You can just set up your tent, move off the grid. It won't cost you nothing. I think they cook up, like, big community meals? In a big pot? People live there all summer. Nobody cares."

"That sounds great. I'll check it out."

"You should definitely check it out." He rips off Ernie's receipt. "If you see Chief, you tell him Danny sent you."

Ernie walks down the winding dirt road back to Portia. For three days he's repeated his drill: he checks the note he's left on the post office bulletin board, as planned; he checks to see if Eva's arrived and left him a note; then he checks the ferry schedule and walks to the terminal to see if she drives off the latest arrival. Today there's no ferry or cruise ships at the pier. When they are there, towering over the docks, visible from the hill at the top of town, the main street pulses with visitors. Today the downtown stores and streets are all shut. Ernie checks the post office. Then he walks down the main street between closed tourist shops and restaurants. He stares in through the windows of one empty bar, and then another, and considers going in. Instead he walks to a convenience store, buys a six-pack, and starts walking back to the campground.

Back at the campsite, Ernie breaks off two beer cans and drinks them quickly while cooking a can of soup on his camp stove. The sun bursts through everything again, heats Ernie up, and fills him with a sense of acceptance. Eva's not coming, he thinks. I'm just kidding myself. He gets up, packs up his pack, and starts walking to the secret campsite. The trail behind the showers is well tracked, but the branches close in around Ernie; soon his backpack and arms are soaked with water from the early rain. In twenty minutes he smells a smoldering campfire. Five minutes later a stronger smell fills his nostrils, like mulch or wet wool. Ernie enters an encampment of squat sheds made of plywood and blue tarps. Three people stand around the smoky fire ring. One is heavyset, easily twice Ernie's mass. He has a long beard and wears a wide-brimmed hat with a bite taken out of the brim, a tie-dyed shirt, and boots with no socks. A pistol is strapped in a holster around his waist. When he sees Ernie approaching, he puts his hand on the pistol.

"How you doing?" Ernie asks. "I'm looking for Chief."

"Oh, yeah?" the heavy one says. "Who's looking for him?"

Ernie doesn't take his eyes off the pistol. "Danny said I should talk to a guy named Chief about maybe camping out here for a little bit, that it would be okay."

"Never heard about nobody named Danny."

The other two, hungrier, elbow each other.

"I mean the ranger. Back there at the campground?"

"Never heard of no Ranger Danny," Chief says. The other two burst out laughing.

"Okay, then," Ernie says, turning slowly. "Sorry to bother you."

"No bother," Chief says. "Free country."

"Okay. Take it easy."

Ernie follows the trail back to his site and sets up camp again. The hobbit bus and its contents have disappeared. Ernie sits on the soaked bench and opens another beer. He pulls his damp wallet out of his damp pocket and counts the bills. Then he counts the days and the days and the days.

Ernie makes his way to
the Foggy Bottom

The next day Ernie walks into the Foggy Bottom. It has huge picture windows and decaying stuffed animal heads. He sits down at the end of a row of stationary locals, all silently nursing shot glasses and bottles. Behind them, a pool table and a jukebox, chairs and tables rest in the shadows under a thin layer of dust. Through the steamy glass, Ernie watches a cruise ship unload dozens of retirees who shuffle up and down the narrow streets, peering into windows. The women wear wide-brimmed safari hats; the men wear naval baseball caps with gold trim and boat insignias. They move from store to store in white sneakers, buying T-shirts or postcards.

On his fifth beer, Ernie is overwhelmed by the smell of human waste. A fat hand places a photograph in front of him. The blurred close-up shows a grizzly bear standing in a stream, clamping down on the back of a salmon. Ernie turns to see a red face with a beard, grinning, the upper front teeth missing. A thick arm presses on the back of the stool.

"What do you think of that?" the man asks, pointing to the bear. "I had to hightail it out of there in a hurry. That bear was sure pissed to see me."

"That's something," Ernie says.

"How you doin'? Name's Ron," he says. "I'm a professional nature photographer. I hitched up here in the spring of '76, and I just never went back. So you want to buy the picture? It's one of my best. Just five bucks."

"No, thanks," Ernie says. "Thanks though."

"I got a couple in here. What do you like. Eagles? Wolf? I got a wolf in here someplace."

Ron rummages through a dog-eared portfolio with one hand, never moving the other from the back of Ernie's stool. He pulls out photos of bears, of eagles, of moose.

"Where the hell's that wolf?" he says. "Well, screw it. You see anything you like? They're all five bucks."

"No, thanks."

Ron removes his arm and starts putting the photos back.

"Yeah. Seven years." He looks down the bar where his empty beer bottle and shot glass sit in a puddle. "Had a job, a house, a wife, a kid. Downland, in the city, you know. Didn't even know what I had there. Then one day I just went for it, just left. And now here I am. A freaking self-employed nature photographer." He turns to Ernie again. "So you coming or going?"

"I'm waiting for a friend."

"Hey, okay. Nice talking. You change your mind, me and my photos are around."

Ernie turns again to look out the window. Eva walks past. She startles him, those huge black curls, those wide brown eyes. But she's walking alongside a man. Ernie's heart drops.

"Eva," Ernie calls from the door. He hesitates, then jostles through the crowd. A block later, he catches up. "Eva!"

"I don't believe it!" She gives Ernie an awkward hug.

"Hey," Ernie says, turning to shake the man's hand. He is very good looking. His black hair is cut neatly, and he has a short beard. He's wearing a new Gore-Tex anorak with a hood, matching rain pants, and new boots. "How you doing?"

"You must be Ernie," the man says. "Eva's told me so much about you."

"This is David," Eva says.

Another wave of retirees comes down the sidewalk, forcing them off the curb. They return to the Foggy Bottom. They sit next to the pool tables and order a pitcher. Eva looks at Ernie. Ernie realizes how bad he must look. He hasn't showered or shaved in days. He feels damp and itchy. Everything he's wearing is soggy.

"David is my friend," she says, putting her hand gently on David's shoulder, "from home. He decided to make the drive with me."

"Yeah," David says. "I just figured she was going to be on the road for a long time, and I was off for a week, so I decided, what the heck."

"I wish you had another week," Eva says.

"Yeah," David says. "Me too. There's just so much energy up here. But hey. I've got to call somebody. I'll be right back." David goes to the far end of the bar to use a pay phone.

"It's so great he could make the trip up with me," Eva says. "After your phone call, I don't know. I just got this incredible energy, I just decided to go for it. But it would have been so scary alone. And David is so supportive, you know. So supportive."

"That's great."

"So David needs to get on the ferry tomorrow. I know this sounds crazy. He needs to get back downland."

"Okay," Ernie says. "I set up camp this morning at the municipal campground. I'm the only one there, I'm sure you can set up there too. It's really nice, right on the cove. If it stops raining—"

"Actually I think David's getting us a hotel room right now."

"Oh," Ernie says. "Yeah, of course."

"It's just that we've been sleeping on the boat deck for three days, and we need showers."

"Of course."

"You can stay there too. I'm sure they've got room."

"That's okay," Ernie says. "I'm all set."

"Cool. After we drop him off tomorrow, we can figure out what we're doing. Okay?"

"Okay."

"It's so great to see you," Eva says. "I'm so glad you're here."

They agree to meet again in two hours for dinner. David and Eva go to their hotel. Ernie stays and finishes the pitcher. The nature photographer gets up from his stool, stumbles toward him, and leans on the chair where David was sitting.

"S'that the friend you was waiting for?" Ron asks.

"Yeah."

"She's very pretty."

"Yes, she is."

Ernie buys a pint and walks the mile down to the waterfront docks. He sits on a pier, watching a long black cruise ship struggle to turn around. The narrow channel bobs with weather-beaten fishing trawlers. The visibility is obscured by low rips of clouds. Gulls scream all around him. The tide drains out of the channel, exposing the cold black tar underneath. The smell of sea marsh and salty air is overpowering. The cruise ship makes a wide turn, blows its horn, and slips south toward the lower forty-eight. Ernie finishes the bottle. He considers walking straight for his tent, crawling in, and forgetting everything, but as he follows the shoreline back through the fog, lights glow from Portia's center. He was supposed to meet Eva and David for dinner after they took showers. It was probably a long time ago. They're probably long gone, Ernie thinks. In which case I'll have a nightcap.

The Foggy Bottom has transformed into a smoky, swirling carnival of light. Christmas lights are strung across the ceiling. Fluorescent beer logos glow from every wall. Groups of six or ten people in parkas adorned with college logos, younger cruise ship passengers testing the local watering hole, cluster noisily around tables covered with overflowing ashtrays and empty pitchers of beer. Locals, men with beards and hip waders and flannels, crowd closer to the bar. Ernie finds an opening at the bar and orders a tequila and a Bud. The lime slice is withered and coated in brown specks.

"There you are!" somebody yells from a table. It's David, alone. He claps Ernie on the back. "We didn't know where you went off to; we checked your campsite and everyplace. Eva went back to the hotel; she's exhausted from the trip. Are you sure you don't want to come stay there? There's vacancies. Hot showers."

"That's okay," Ernie says.

"I'm headed back tomorrow," David says, swaying a little. "I'm really excited to be here though. I'm really glad I came."

"I'm sure Eva really appreciates it."

"Well, my fiancée talked me into it, actually," David says. "She thought it was a good idea for me to get away for a bit, and she's quite fond of Eva. They're good friends."

"Oh," Ernie says. "Your fiancée."

"Yes," David says. He quickly pulls a photograph of a pensive brunette out of his wallet. She's wearing a beret and standing in front of a mountain lake, barely smiling. David looks down at her and chuckles to himself. "Ah, Jenny," he says. "I was just on the phone with her. I've called her every day for two weeks. Every day we had a phone. There's no phone on the ferry."

"Yeah," Ernie says. "That makes sense."

"Well," David says. "Can I get you a beer?" Ernie listens to David for some time, telling him about Jenny—she's a poet, she doesn't like camping, her vision and energy are great. Jenny felt David really needed to do this, to see Eva up the road on her journey. David goes on, but for Ernie, the room is spinning behind him. The lights and the voices and the noise and the smoke all twirl concentrically behind his head, around the pool tables. A stuffed moose bobs its head. Ernie is rooted on the spot, his legs heavy, gripping the beer, rocking back and forth.

"Eva's told me so much about you," David says. "She's really been looking forward to—"

"Hey, man," Ernie says. "Shoot some pool?"

"Pool?" David says. "I'm afraid I'm not very good."

"Okay," Ernie says. "I'm going to shoot a game."

Ernie beats a red parka with a pair of late bank shots. Next up is a blue parka. He's a hacker. Ernie puts him down in two rounds, walking the eight ball the length of the table. "You've played some pool, young fellow," an older yellow parka says loudly from one of the tables. On the pool table, the vectors come together, each shot lining up perfectly behind the other. One person scratches on the eight ball, another leaves all his balls on the table. One buys Ernie a beer, another claps him on the back.

Ernie holds the table for ten games. The bus taking the cruise ship passengers back to the dock arrives at midnight. They file out suddenly, leaving a handful of locals at the bar. Ernie puts the cue down and walks to David, who is slouched next to the nature photographer, a row of empty beer bottles in front of them both. He is holding his picture of Jenny.

"She's so great, she's everything to me," David slurs. "You know what I mean?"

The photographer looks down at his wildlife photos, spread out in front of David, soaking in spilled beer. "Yeah," he says. "I know what you mean."

Geographically, the Grizzle Peninsula is relatively young; it is believed to have been twisted, ripped, and dragged from the mainland during the last ice age. But even before then, there are indicators that the mountain crags that stick up like 10,000-foot teeth along the western coast served as a strong barrier that preserved unique and ancient plant life, trees, and wildlife that became extinct or evolved on the mainland. At the time of this writing, very little research has been conducted on the plants and animals that populate the wilderness, much of which has yet to be explored. In the absence of research are spectacular legends of wild beasts and quick-mud, of hidden civilizations and wild men hunting in the forests.

In truth, the Grizzle Peninsula was traveled by humans for thousands of years who adapted and innovated to survive its harsh climate, and who made full use of its generous resources. Western explorers stumbled upon the Grizzle Peninsula during the age of exploration when Sir John Clarke became lost in the winter ice floes seeking a northwest passage and, in a dense fog, ran his sailboat and thirty crewmen aground just off the coast of what is now the city of Petrolia, on the eastern shore, in 1560. "A cold and desolate land," he wrote in his journal, "bereft of all life and nourifhment, poure of soille, cruelle to the bodie and to the ey." After frantically repairing their ship, Sir John sailed home for England, never to explore again.

A century later, others tried to map the region, but found the coast impossible in its shrouds of fog and perilous shoals, and the forest and mountains impenetrable. Many expeditions disappeared altogether. In the late 1700s, an ultra-orthodox religious sect sailed for "Utopia" and created, briefly, a settlement somewhere in the farthest reaches of the Grizzle Peninsula. As legend has it, they built a cathedral in the wilderness, surrounded by magnificent houses. Boats brought more settlers for ten years; then, suddenly, the boats and any indications of life stopped, the settlement crushed by yellow fever. Loggers and prospectors found the forests too deep and the soil too poor for their purposes and returned home empty-handed.

Fishing was always rich in the warm waters swirling up from the west, and in 1900, the first fishing settlements were established in Portia. A small but determined group of pioneers carved a small town out of the wilderness, and despite a huge toll in human life from the unforgiving sea, they managed to build an industry. Farther up the east coast, oil was discovered, leading to development of what is now Petrolia. Small settlements started carving little niches deeper into the forests, interconnected by woodland trails. As with the last wilderness areas disappearing from the rest of the world, the twentieth century would probably have been cruel to this wild, untouched region, if not for the Great Panic in the early days of the Second World War, and the sudden arrival of the more panicked military.

Soon after Pearl Harbor, the occupation of several unpopulated islands off the Grizzle Peninsula by enemy forces suggested an upcoming invasion along the coast. In 1942, while millions of soldiers and resources were committed elsewhere overseas, the Army sent several engineering battalions racing to the Grizzle Peninsula to carve roads for supply lines through the wilderness and to build bases and fortifications on the rare strips of beach where an invasion might be possible. The resulting Soldier's Highway was created, winding from the mainland highway to Portia and then up to Petrolia. While better-trained, better-prepared engineer battalions worked the road up to Portia, the Army had to find new laborers to build the harder sections—from Portia to Petrolia and beyond—in the winter of 1942, remembered as the most severe in decades. Assigned to this task were prison soldiers from southern penitentiaries. The job was performed hastily and at great loss of life, with prisoner soldiers freezing to death in droves and whole battalions disappearing into the wilds. Survivors were assured that their sentences would be revoked on completion; that they would be handed military weapons and sent to fight alongside the soldiers. This never happened; the few who survived the harsh conditions and winter were sent back to their prisons when the Great Panic fizzled out and the war moved on. The legend of a lost battalion, where whole teams of soldiers vanished into the woods and may still survive today, is a big part of the region's folklore. Traces of trails, military equipment, and supplies are scattered throughout the western spine of mountains from Portia to the Great Gulf wilderness and beyond, but it is unlikely that groups of soldiers remain wandering the forests today.

After the war, for thirty years in military circles, a one-year assignment to the Grizzle Peninsula was referred to as the "Big Question." The peninsula is shaped like a question mark; however, for the military personnel who suffered long, boring, uncomfortable months in bitterly freezing winter conditions, the question mark often accompanied the question, "Why are we here?" The military occupation of the peninsula was in many ways a Cold War dinosaur; after an early (but never-realized) panic of invasion necessitated the fast construction of Grizzle's road, airstrips, and bases, which dotted the mainland and islands, ten thousand sad souls in uniform settled in for an uneasy sleep, unable even to complain to their mothers and sweethearts about the desperate meaninglessness of their secretive post.

The Great Panic subsided, but the Army remained. Petrolia became a military city with increasing numbers of contractors brought up for oil extraction, a practice that was limited until today. The population of the entire Grizzle Peninsula stayed steady for thirty years, at five thousand military personnel and approximately five thousand civilians, a population estimated at one person for every one hundred square miles. Time passed quietly; outside of Petrolia, world developments like the telephone, television, and jet travel barely reached the people of Grizzle. A major volcano in 1972 threatened, but did not harm, Petrolia; it did, however, cut off the little dirt road winding beyond it, and any settlements that may have existed there.

The aforementioned legislation that passed in 1975 and the wider reaching openings in 1982, which opened up the peninsula to the public, did not settle well with many locals used to their way of life in the wilderness; for others it has opened open opportunities to make money from tourism and the possibility of much larger development in the years ahead.

Ernie and Eva wake up
to rain

Ernie and Eva wake up to a third day of rain. They scramble to the car, pulling the tent down quickly, but it's too late; their sleeping bags and their clothes are soaked. They drive slowly along the mud track for hours, across waterlogged tundra, between clumps of short trees. Something glitters in the wilderness—a stainless steel diner, like a railroad car dropped in the middle of a dark forest. It sits in the woods just off the road, surrounded by a dozen smoky log cabins. Two logging trucks and a pickup truck are parked out front. Eva and Ernie run from the car across a muddy parking lot, enter, and sit at the counter. Eva reaches into her pockets.

"What's wrong?" Ernie asks.

"I forgot something," Eva says, rising from her stool.

Ernie watches Eva cross the parking lot. A waitress comes from the kitchen. Ernie looks at a row of glistening Budweiser bottles in a case behind the counter; he hasn't had a beer in three days. He could easily drink all twelve.

"What will you have?" the waitress asks.

"I'll have a coffee, please," Ernie says. "And a tea for my friend." In the parking lot, Eva's boots stick out from the driver's seat. She pulls something out of her glove compartment. She puts it back. She digs out a few dollar bills, then tucks them into her back pocket. She reaches back to organize something in the back seat. She gets out of the car, shuts the door, and walks slowly toward the steps.

Eva sits down on the stool. The silence continues. She hasn't looked at him since they left Portia three days ago. Her face is creased with a frown; it's as dark as the smile he remembers, he longs for, was bright. Particles of water cling to her black trusses, to her ragg wool shoulders.

"What were you looking for?" Ernie asks.

"Nothing," she answers.

"I ordered you a tea."

"Tea will be nice." The rain batters the roof of Eva's car. She takes a deep breath.

"I was just thinking about David," she says.

"David? Oh." Ernie watches the waitress carry two beer bottles to a pair of huge men at the other end of the counter. They drop forks from large plates of roast beef and gravy. They laugh, tap the bottles together, and chug. Ernie swallows the last of his coffee.

"David was my navigator. Back at the institute."

"The institute?" Ernie says. "What institute?"

"The institute. I only knew David a short time there, but we became really good friends. We knew each other from a past life. I just know it."

"How do you know it?" Ernie asks.

"Well," Eva says, "it's like this. It's like, sometimes you just see somebody and you say, 'There he is,' like you've known him your whole life, or her, you just know. It's like the first time I saw him there, standing on the steps of the institute, smiling, and I just got, like, this major tingling. Like I knew him before."

"Oh," Ernie says.

"Sometimes you just know it. I just know it, that's all." Eva squints at her car. "Like each time I saw him, I felt this major tingling? I know you can't understand that, but the people who practice what I'm about, and what I believe in, are just tuned in to it. And it manifests itself in so many ways. So many ways. And like, at the institute we, well — I don't know. It's difficult to explain. I'll try though. When you're ready."

"Okay."

"David is cool though. Definitely cool."

"Yeah," Ernie says. "Cool."

Two hours later, they drive up a pass between luminous peaks. Eva stares blankly over the wheel. Ernie slouches in the passenger seat, focusing on the landscape disappearing in the half-shattered mirror. Ernie's thinking, trying to remember. He remembers that he said something to her on the phone, something that got her to climb into her car and travel three thousand miles to be here. Now here they were. What had he said?

"Okay," Eva starts again, drawing a deep breath. "I'll try to explain it. It's like manifesting? Manifesting is a skill I learned at the institute. It's not a secret power. It's not like hokey pokey, it's not like new-agey fuzzy-wuzzy or any of that stuff. It's a skill we all have, only we don't, you know, even know it."

"Manifesting," Ernie says.

"Yes. Like in group, we were taught that we all have these powers to make anything happen, and it can be anything you want. So, what happened was that David brought us together one day and explained to us how we could focus on something, and it could be anything, like a bike, like a hundred dollars, like a new watch, like anything you want."

A funny whining noise, barely discernable over the squeak of the windshield wipers, starts singing from the engine.

"David's not like a cult guy or something, you know? He's really down to earth. You'd probably like him." The noise grows louder. "So David taught us a series of focus practices, concentrations, called Ashrasha. Ashrasha is so cool. You feel your energies rising up from your core. It's how we learn to heal ourselves and others. I'll explain this to you, or maybe not — it's pretty deep stuff. And so now, through

Ashrasha, we came together as a group, all of the women in the group, and we focused on what we really wanted. Roberta really wanted a bike so bad, and Wendy really needed eighty-six dollars to pay her phone bill, and all I wanted was a long-stemmed rose."

"Ashrasha," Ernie says. The engine is clanking now. Something slaps itself repeatedly.

"And do you know what happened the next day! The next day!" Eva's yelling now, pounding her palms against the steering wheel. "Wendy found eighty-six dollars in a brown paper bag lying on the street outside Alfalfa's! Like, eighty-six exactly! And Roberta ran into this guy she used to know, and she hadn't seen him in a million zillion years, and he said to her, 'Hey, like I'm moving. You want my bike?' And I found a rose on the sidewalk!"

"Yeah, wow," Ernie says.

"Oh, crap!"

"Yeah," Ernie says. "Crap."

"No, crap! Look at the heat gauge!" Beneath the scratched, bent plastic covering of the car's instrument panel, an arrow presses red-hot. "Oh, crap! We gotta pull over."

Eva pulls over into a gravel bowl with no guardrails. A steep embankment hurtles down into a silt-filled creek. Ernie climbs out and pulls up the hood of the car. He stands with his hands on his hips, looking at the engine.

"Oh, crap, crap, crap." Eva bangs her head on the steering wheel. Eventually she climbs out and stands next to him. Ernie pulls on the fan belt, black and charred and tangled.

"Do you know what you're doing?" Eva asks.

Ernie remembers three guys he knew in high school. They spent Saturday nights with a case of beer in their dads' garages, dismantling and rebuilding car engines. They started inviting him over. He tried to look cool, drank beer, and occasionally handed somebody a socket wrench. One of them got killed in a wreck, Ernie remembers. One ended up in jail. One's selling used cars.

"Do you know what you're doing?" Eva asks again.

Ernie pulls hard enough so the band snaps. He holds it up to show her.

"I think it's this thing," he says.

Eva climbs back in the car, rolls up the window, sits back in the front seat, and closes her eyes. Ernie tries tying a knot in the charred belt. Little pieces snap off in his fingers. He looks up at the ledges above them. Black clouds pour through the cracks. The rain starts again. Ernie climbs into the passenger seat.

"Why don't we try going," he says.

Eva takes a deep breath. "Because we don't have a fan belt."

"Why don't we go until the heat gauge rises, then stop until it cools off, then go again?"

Eva turns the ignition. The engine groans. The heat meter rises slowly as they climb to the crest of the ridge. As they pass through a cut between boulders at the top of the ridge, the sky opens up, flashing a halo of blue light on black and silver cliffs, drenched in sweat and steam and mist. Then the black clouds seal together. Eva turns the engine off, and they roll down the notch into a deep fog. After four hairpin turns, the road flattens out. A hand-painted sign reading "INN" appears, drawing them up a steep driveway. They roll into a parking space between two tour buses and the motor stalls.

Ernie walks into a large dining hall. Behind a desk sits a small man with thick glasses, a pressed flannel shirt, and a well-trimmed beard. Behind him, teenage waiters scramble to serve lunch to the busloads of tourists.

"Excuse me, sir," Ernie says. "I'm having a little car trouble. Do you have a wrench I can borrow?"

The innkeeper snorts. "Zachary?" he says to one of the kids hurrying by.

"Yes, sir?"

"This person needs a wrench. Can you bring me my toolbox?"

"Yes, sir."

The man selects a wrench and hands it to Ernie. "Bring it back," he says.

"I will, yes, sir," Ernie says. "I'll be sure to."

"What are you going to do with that?" Eva asks when she sees the wrench.

Ernie says nothing. He pops open the hood and stands in the drizzle, struggling to restrap the fan belt to the motor with the wrench handle. Eva shakes her head, then goes inside. She sits in the dining hall with a cup of tea, frowning at Ernie through the window. Ernie can see someone sitting alone at the table next to her. A man with long hair, a droopy mustache. A long, hairy forearm holds a coffee mug. The man says something. Eva shrugs and laughs. Ernie bangs his knuckles against the radiator, peeling the skin. The inn door opens behind him. He hopes it's Eva with a six-pack. He turns to see the man with the droopy mustache.

"How's it going?" the man asks.

"Not so good."

The man pulls a flask from his pocket, takes a pull, and hands it to Ernie.

"Here," he says. "This'll heat you up."

"Don't mind if I do," Ernie says. The contents explode in his sinuses, like burning caramel. It's the first thing he's really tasted in three days.

"Can I take a look at it?" the man asks, pointing to the engine.

"Yeah, sure. I'd appreciate it."

"Just a minute, let me get my toolbox out of my plane," he says. "I'll be right back. Help yourself to that." He struts around the corner of the building.

Ernie holds the flask tightly to his chest, then takes another long pull. He looks back up at Eva in the window. She's staring down into her cup.

"So it's the water pump," Ernie says thirty minutes later, standing in front of Eva's table. He clenches the wrench in one black hand, wipes the other against his pants.

"What does that mean?" Eva says.

"It seized up. The water pump. That's why the belt burned. We got to get a new one."

Ernie looks out the window at the man with the droopy mustache putting his tools away in the rain. "He's a real nice guy," Ernie says. "He's a bush pilot. He was flying back from dropping off some fisherman, and he got socked in. There's a little airstrip out back. He's going to wait it out."

Eva crinkles her nose. "Have you been drinking?" she asks.

"He's a nice guy. He showed me how to change the pump."

"Great."

Ernie wipes the wrench handle clean before taking it back to the innkeeper, who examines it carefully.

"Can you tell me where the nearest garage is?" Ernie asks. The innkeeper points down the road. "Can you tell me how far?"

"Eighty miles," he says. "Smitty's Auto."

"Can I use your phone?"

"There's a pay phone over there," the innkeeper says, still looking at his wrench. "Anybody can use it."

When Ernie returns to the table. Eva's speaking with a waiter.

"So there's a garage, eighty miles up," he says. "Smitty's Auto. I can hitch up there, buy the pump and the belt. S'better if just one of us goes. I'll be back in a few hours."

"It's going to be dark in a few hours," Eva says. "Did you call them? Do they have the pump?"

"No answer."

"There's a campsite just up the dirt road," the waiter whispers to Eva, watching the innkeeper. "You guys could camp up there. He never checks up there."

Eva and Ernie pull the car into a little clearing behind the inn. The rain has broken down into a cold spray. Across an open strip, they can barely make out the little plane in the fog, the pilot sleeping behind the condensation on the windshield.

"I should go," Eva says, pulling the damp tarp from the well of the back seat. "You don't know what you're doing."

"I know what I'm doing," Ernie says.

"How do you know that's what we need? How do you know we need a water pump? What if you hitchhike down there and buy it and hitchhike all the way back, and it's not what we need?"

"Because that's what your pal there, Mister Bush Pilot, told me we needed."

"What do you know? What do you know about cars? You don't know anything about cars. And you're drunk. I should go down there."

"We need a water pump," Ernie says. "I need to go buy a water pump."

"You don't even know what a water pump is."

"Well, since we need one so bad," Ernie says, "why don't you just manifest one?"

Eva blinks at him, then bursts into tears. She folds her arms tightly in front of her, shaking her shaggy head back and forth.

"I knew you wouldn't understand," she whispers. "I knew I shouldn't try."

"I better get going. I'll be back in a couple hours."

At six o'clock, a pickup truck drops Ernie across from Smitty's Auto Garage. Truck and auto carcasses litter the dark woods. At the side of a weathered barn, an elderly man in grease-caked overalls rummages through the engine of a rusted wreck of a truck. His head submerged beneath, he bellows as he pulls clumps of mud and grass out from somewhere deep in the well of the engine.

"Crap!" he yells. "Jesus! Crap!"

"Hello," Ernie says. The old man rises very slowly from the engine and turns to Ernie, wiping his black hands on his pants.

"Hello there."

Ernie holds out the water pump and the belt. "Our car broke down up the road, at the inn," Ernie says. "It's the pump. Is for a '76 Datsun wagon. Do you have a pump?"

"I don't, no."

"Can you tell me where I might get one?"

"There's an auto parts store down in Cabbage, another sixty miles down the road," the old man says. "I'm pretty sure it closes in an hour though."

At nine o'clock, a dirt-caked sedan drops Ernie off in front of the closed auto parts store. The lights are out, but Ernie taps on the door for fifteen minutes. It starts to rain again. The settlement of Cabbage folds out into the woods all around him, plywood homes with floodlights staining the black mist, the dark horizon marked with telephone wires and jagged forest. Across the parking lot, Ernie sees glowing Miller beer signs. Motorcycles are parked in a row in front of the bar door. Alongside the bar is a motel. The rain starts pelting him, and he starts running.

The bar is empty except for the bartender, a pockmarked older woman whose hair is hacked short in the front and on the sides and feathered in the back. She wears a sleeveless black T-shirt. On a wide-screen TV, two deformed sociopaths chase a helpless young girl through the woods. The girl screams every fifteen seconds. The bartender barely removes her eyes from the screen. She pours Ernie a draft beer. She picks up the phone.

"Well, what's he doing?" she shouts. "Well, tell him to shut up then."

She lights a long white cigarette. In the movie, the teenager gets chased from a log cabin by a walking corpse. Then, for some mysterious reason, she turns around and goes back into the cabin. The bartender pours Ernie another beer.

"I seen this here movie a hundred times," she says.

"How much is a room for the night?"

"Sixty dollars," she says. "Hardly worth it. 'Less you're desperate."

"Where are the people who own the bikes out there?"

"Who the hell knows? Out raising hell someplace."

Ernie drinks for a long time, not sure if he's paying for every beer or every other beer. The movie drifts into another. The woman moves across the bar. Nobody else enters or leaves.

Ernie tries to remember talking to Eva, but he can't. He remembered talking to her on the phone about coming up here. He was going for it; she wanted to go for it, but there were people, she told him, who didn't want her to go for it. Then she went for it. But she didn't entirely go for it. It was all very confusing, Ernie thought, but that was that, and here we are.

He wasn't sober the last time he called her, he admits to himself—he was very, very drunk when he called her—but the memory of Eva's smile, the pay phone, then the newspaper sitting before him, all start blurring, swirling around in front of Ernie. He looks up. The bartender lady is gone. The TV screen is a sea of gray snow. Some of the lights are off. Was he sleeping? He remembers the motorcycles. He walks to the door, but it's bolted, apparently from the outside. A dog howls somewhere.

Ernie thinks of Eva, 140 miles up the mountain, in a campsite, alone. She came three thousand miles to meet him up here. She left her home, her friends, her world to be with him. Now he's screwed everything up. Now her car is dead, and she's waiting for him, just a couple of bucks left in her pocket. She's lying in her tent, stranded, alone and fragile in the dark in the wilderness, squeezing her eyes shut, trying to make something happen.

Ernie tries the door again but can't get it to budge. He checks the windows, which are padlocked shut. He walks into the men's room. He looks up at a narrow window. He jimmies it open, knowing he'll never be able to hoist himself up there, then does so with ease. He pulls himself through the little gap, feeling his ribs, his gaunt stomach, his bony hips, bones, and muscle he had no idea he had three months before, slide through the opening with ease. I must have lost thirty pounds on this trip, he thinks as he slips out and hurtles headfirst toward the ground. He falls flat on his back into the empty parking lot. I'll bet it's thirty, he thinks, lying there. I should really get on a scale, check it out. He remembers the bikes and the bolted door, pulls himself up, and slips back toward the center of Cabbage.

*

At eight o'clock the next morning, Ernie's back out on the highway, hunched against the cold, holding the water pump in an auto parts bag. He stomps his feet and watches the sun rise over a row of pine trees. A station wagon with a smashed windshield appears. The license plates have "WWII POW" emblazoned above the numbers. The wagon pulls off the pavement, into the mud at Ernie's feet, and he climbs in. The interior is coated in brown silt. Tools and pipes clang in the backseat well. Next to Ernie, an old man hunches over the steering wheel trying to peer through the cracks in the windshield.

"I don't normally pick up no hitchers," the old man says. "But it's freezing out."

Ernie looks at the bag sitting in his lap. "Had a little car trouble," he says.

"Ain't none of my business. Now I'm only going up to the crossroad, but that'll get you up the road a short ways and give you a chance to warm up a spell. Where'd you spend the night?"

"I found a shed," Ernie says. The old man snorts.

"That's my gear back there. I been digging wells up here more'n thirty years. Since the war."

"You in the war?"

"Didn't you see them license plates I've got up there when you got in the car? Territory gave me them plates. Them there's prisoner of war veteran's plates. I was in the war over there and then the one over here, in the islands. Nobody never talks about the war over here. They call it the Great Panic? If they'd been there on that beach, they'd know what panic was. That's where them bastards got me in one of them prisoner of war camps. Two years. After that I came back up here."

"Wow," Ernie says.

"Yep. I get to park anywhere I want with them plates."

"You've seen some changes," Ernie says.

"You wouldn't believe it. I built a house up Mountain View Road there thirty years ago, me and the wife. Now we're surrounded by houses. Which wouldn't be so bad, so long as people minded to their own affairs and took care of their own dogs."

"Dogs?" Ernie asks. He remembers hearing howling the night before.

"Yeah, all these newcomers, they come up here buying dogs. But nobody knows how to take care of them! So they run all over the place attacking everything. They tore my yard to shreds. They tore up my garbage, attacked my dog, scared the hell out of my wife. I told them folks to tie up their damn dogs, but they don't listen. I called the sheriff, but he don't do nothing.

"Then one night a bunch of them dogs got into my livestock, my chickens. So I went out and shot two of them and carried the bodies up to the owners' houses and left them on the porch. That got the sheriff hollering at me. I had to go to court. I had to pay a fine. A hundred dollars—a hundred dollars because I was protecting my chickens! Then the next bunch of folks let their dogs go, and they come after my chickens, and I done the same thing, and it cost me two hundred dollars. The thing is, I don't want to do it. It ain't the damn dogs' fault. It's the people who got the dogs who don't know how to keep them from running wild. Given the chance, I'd rather shoot the people. Only I know better. So last night I heard more dogs out back. I called the sheriff. Only the sheriff said he wasn't coming all the way out there to Mountain View Road, not for no dogs. 'Well, then,' I said, 'I'll shoot 'em again,' I told the sheriff. 'Well, that'll cost you five hundred dollars this time,' said the sheriff. 'Well, go to hell,' I told the sheriff, and I hung up.

"We're coming to the crossroads now," he interrupts himself. "That's where I'm digging this here well. There's a pull-off where you're most likely to git a ride. Should be lots of folks headed back downland this time of year."

"So what did you do about the dogs?" Ernie asks.

"Well, last night, I showed 'em. I didn't shoot the dogs. Instead I backed the wagon out to the chicken coop with the tailgate open and a plate of hamburgers in the back. When the dogs got in the back there, I shut the door and drove them down to the sheriff's office. I knew the sheriff left the office doors open all night. So I ran the dogs in there at three in the morning, threw a couple more hamburgers in there, and shut the door behind me."

The old man bursts into giggles. He slams his palms on the steering wheel, sending the wagon lurching, then pulls up slowly in front of a general store with a bucketful of red roses sitting by the door. The old man turns to Ernie, beaming, his eyes sparkling like a child's.

"Say, right about now," he says, laughing, "won't that sheriff be in for a surprise?"

At noon, Ernie jumps off a flatbed logging truck. He runs across the driveway, past the inn, up the dirt road to the campsite. Eva is still there, but where else could she be? She sits on a log by the tent, staring off into space. When she sees him, she stands up.

"I was so worried," she says.

"I was okay," he says.

"But then I had this major tingling, and I knew it. I just knew it."

Ernie reaches into the bag and pulls out a single long-stemmed rose.

"What's this for?" she asks.

"It's for being sorry," he says.

"Well, that was a waste of money," she says, and she turns away from him. But as she does, Ernie thinks he sees the first hint of that smile.

Ernie and Eva climb
over a guardrail

Ernie and Eva climb over a guardrail. A narrow trail descends through huge, dripping ferns. Strange smells—smoke, sewage, steak sauce—float between the trees. The trail opens onto a stony cove. Beyond it is a green glacial lake, then luminous blue slopes, distant, cut by trenches of snow. The far shoreline is piled high with shattered tree trunks and boulders. Climbing over a fallen log, Eva slips; instinctively, Ernie puts his arm out to catch her. She pushes his arm away quickly.

"Thanks," Eva says.

"Sure," Ernie says.

Ernie sets up the tent, then builds a fire. Eva pulls her damp poncho out of her pack and spreads it over her legs. She brushes mud and dead leaves from its surface.

"What a beautiful spot," Ernie says.

Eva looks up at the mountains, then back down at her poncho, and shrugs.

"You've become quite an expert on beauty," she says. "This is beautiful. That's beautiful. It's all you've said for three weeks."

"Don't you think this is beautiful?" Ernie asks.

Eva focuses on the dead leaves.

Ernie throws a branch on the fire. He's startled by a small man standing on the shoreline twenty yards away. The man is wearing a blue turban.

"Greetings to you!" he yells as he approaches.

"Beautiful spot," Ernie says.

The man squints up at the ledges. "It is—how do you say it? Treacherous."

Ernie scans the shoreline for another tent. "Are you camping near here?" he asks.

"Here? No. Actually I just bought a trailer. Actually it is just over there." He points down the shoreline at the woods. "Actually it is a park full of trailers."

"Wow," Ernie says. "What a beautiful place for a trailer park."

"Yes, I suppose. If one likes such things."

Eva puts her poncho down. She pulls out her crumpled sleeping bag, sweater, and clothing, and spreads them out on the rocks to dry.

"Yes," the man continues. "I came here two months ago, you see. Two months. I am a McDonald's store manager. I have just started managing a McDonald's store. In downtown Petrolia. Yes. Not very far from here, you see. It is my twelfth McDonald's store in the last eleven years. I move to them, I manage them, I move again. This is what I do, you see. This way, I see things. Now I see all of this."

The man gestures gently toward the landscape, then turns, his hands out for balance, stepping gingerly on flat leather sandals.

"Yes, well," he says. "It is good to meet you. You stop by the McDonald's and give your greetings."

He works his way back along the shoreline. As he scrambles up into the woods and disappears, Eva says, "Now that's a man who knows where he wants to go in life."

Darkness seeps into everything. Ernie tries to make the fire bigger. A cold wind presses down the slopes, crosses the lake, and circles them. Eva takes a long breath, then unloads what she'd been alluding to for days as they approached Petrolia: David had told her about his friends and spiritual partners who moved up here five years before, who were wonderful, who would definitely put Eva up, who could help her find work. David had reassured her that she could drop in on their friends, but she didn't know about Ernie, and it wouldn't be cool, not yet, until Eva was set up, or something—you know, maybe they can just work from there. See how it goes. Eva says she can drop Ernie downtown in the morning; he can resupply and hang out at his beautiful lake and figure out what he's doing. Maybe they can reconnect in a few days.

In the morning, Eva and Ernie drive out of the wilderness. Within minutes, they are surrounded by auto parts stores, trailer parks, and warehouses. Eva drops Ernie off on a strip, then drives away. He sits reading a paper on a bench for forty-five minutes, then walks into the first bar he sees. That's that, Ernie says to himself, draining his first beer of the day. No reason not to have another. After a few hours, he walks a few miles, then finds a second bar, then a third. The bars swirl with menacing characters—soldiers, bikers, fishermen—but nothing happens.

When he walks out of the last bar, darkness is falling. Ernie can barely make out the blue ridge of mountains where his tent and belongings are perched by a lake. He starts walking, comes across a McDonald's. He stumbles in. A small man with a green turban and a shadow of a moustache, with a McDonald's manager shirt and tie, blinks at him.

"Can I help you, sir?"

Ernie leans over the counter. "Greetings to you!" Ernie shouts. "Isn't this beautiful?"

Then Ernie remembers. The man last night had a blue turban. And this one is holding a baseball bat.

*

Ernie comes to in a hospital waiting room. He's cradled in a plastic chair, and he's pressing a handful of gauze to his nose. The gauze is brown and dry and sticks to his skin. Two fiberglass doors swing open. "Come with me," a voice says briskly. Ernie follows a nurse in green scrubs into an examining room. She points to a table. Ernie lies down on the white paper.

"Take your shoes off, please," she says.

"Why?" Ernie asks.

"Fine," she says. "Keep them on." She leans over his face. Her hair is tied back tightly, and she wears huge glasses.

"Now, then. What seems to be the problem."

"It's my nose, I think. I think it may be broken."

"Really? May I?" She pulls the gauze away. Something dislodges itself from the cavity between Ernie's eyes. His face fills with a rush of cold air.

"The trooper says he found you walking along the airport road. Do you mind telling me what happened?"

"I got hit with a baseball bat, I think. In a McDonald's."

She wipes Ernie's face. It sears his skin and leaves ticklish little flecks on his cheeks. He's sure his nose is split open.

"Is it broken?" he asks.

"I don't know. Maybe it is. Maybe it isn't."

"Are you going to take an X-ray?"

"Why. Do you think you need an X-ray?"

"If it's broken, don't I need an X-ray?"

"If it's broken, it's broken. You need to know if it's broken? You need an X-ray to tell you it's broken?"

The nurse removes her big glasses and squints, pinching the space between her eyes. She rubs the glasses against the sleeve of her scrub shirt. She squints up at a clock on the other side of the room. Without her glasses, her eyes are so small, Ernie thinks. So small and disappointing.

"Okay," she says. "We need to do some paperwork."

"Am I going to be admitted?"

"I didn't say that."

"Okay."

"Do you want to be admitted?"

Ernie pictures a bed with clean white sheets and a little water pitcher on the table.

"You can get admitted for a broken nose?" he asks.

"I didn't say that either."

"For what then?"

"For observation."

"Really? For how long?"

"Until we've made all our observations."

She examines the paperwork very closely. Then she puts it down. "But my impression is that there's nothing really wrong with you."

Ernie touches his nose. "There isn't?"

"I think the best thing you can do is get right back out there."

"Out there?"

"All you downlanders come up here for some kind of reason. All you downlanders come up here, pretending you're not running away from something, pretending you're going to find something. And, well, guess what." She holds up a hand mirror. Ernie can see a clear bandage over the bridge of his nose. The blood is gone. "You're free to go."

The rain sweeps in again. Ernie follows the guardrail back up the road to the campsite. The glowing lights of Petrolia fade behind him. When he barely makes out Eva's car, parked where they left it the night before, he thinks he's dreaming. He stumbles down the dark, wet trail.

Eva is sitting on the same log by the tent, under a tarp, reading a book with a flashlight.

"What happened to your nose?" she asks.

"I walked into something," Ernie says. He sits on a log across from her. "What happened with your friends?"

"They weren't there," Eva says.

"Well, you can try back tomorrow, right?"

"I talked to their neighbors," she says. "They moved a year ago. Back downland."

"I'm sorry to hear that," Ernie says.

"I drove back to where I dropped you off. I checked everywhere. I must have checked twenty bars. Then I came back here. And you still weren't here."

"Yeah," Ernie says. "Sorry."

Eva waves the meek yellow beam of her flashlight out toward the huge lake and mountains that, in the blackness, now seem to loom over them.

Then she whispers, "You better not leave me here."

Danny and Fiona go
looking for Chief

Danny's name adorns the bronze badge just under his forest service park attendant badge. It never fails that with each nocturnal disruption (all too often someone screams "bear" from the living room of their camper, and Danny, glassy-faced, flashes his flashlight into the eyes of a shrugging raccoon), the complainant will try to read the name on the nameplate, cock his or her large head sideways, mouth the words slowly, and give up. Danny likes it this way; it creates an instant distance between him and the soft elderly people he finds himself surrounded by in this crap-ass campground he's been assigned to. By midsummer the complaints have increased; often the campers come back from day trips and can't find their medications. Danny just shrugs. He came to Grizzle with dreams of an assignment to one of the great national parks. As time passes and the season's end approaches, he only grows more pissed off. He lets his hair shag out and wears his shirt untucked and rarely files the mountains of reports that pile up on his desk.

But on one particular sparkling blue morning, as he struggles to steer the large green park service pickup truck through the campground, he hopes the young woman sitting in his passenger seat—a Fiona Gallagher, from Fish and Game—will ask him about his name plate. Instead she stares intently down at a stack of forms clipped neatly together in her lap and marks certain boxes with a red pen.

"That's an awful lot of paperwork you fish-and-gamers gotta fill out," Danny says.

"You don't have a lot of paperwork at Park Service?" she says without looking up at him.

"I didn't say that," Danny says. "I mean, not exactly. Like, we've got accident reports to fill out all the time, incident reports. Property damage, missing meds. Stuff like that."

The truck hits a rut in the dirt road, reminding Danny to reach for the gear to downshift, but he forgets to step on the clutch. The old truck lurches and squeals like its guts are being ripped out. Danny senses Fiona's head rise for a second, alarmed; her hair so blond it's white, splashing around the cabin next to him like small, sparkling leaves. He hasn't sat next to a girl in a truck in a long time. Well, to be honest, pretty much not at all.

"Sorry about that," he says. "Old truck. Clutch sucks."

"Don't worry about it," she says. She drops the clipboard into the heavy duffel bag at her feet and pulls out an empty leather holster. She leans forward and straps it onto her hip belt.

"What's that for?" Danny says.

"It's for this," Fiona says, pulling a large black revolver from the bag and opening the chamber.

"Do you really think that's necessary?" Danny asks. "I mean, a gun?"

"According to the report, the assailant is armed," Fiona says. "Is that correct?"

"Yeah, but I know who it is," Danny says. "I mean, I'm pretty sure I think I know who it is. And he's harmless."

"He's not that harmless. He shot a bear in the head," she says. "Three people reported a single gunshot. We found the bear in a Dumpster."

Danny pulls the truck up next to the campsite showers. Behind them there's a grove of dense, low-hanging pine boughs.

"This is the trail in," Danny says. "Let's not do anything crazy."

"I'm just going to do my job," Fiona says, loading bullets into the gun's chamber. "And your job is to help me do my job."

"Can you wait to load the gun until I'm out of the truck at least?" Danny says, struggling to pull the keys from the ignition.

"Yeah," Fiona says. "That's probably a good idea."

Fiona leads the way up the trail. Danny tries to focus his eyes on the forest around them. Many of the trunks are dead, the hollow remnants of a fire started when a camper's generator exploded at one of the sites behind them. Danny thought this might be a good point of conversation, to change the topic from Fiona's loaded gun.

"So there was this huge fire here, like ten years ago."

"So how do you know this person?" she asks.

"What person?"

"The person who shot the bear? The one we're going to have a word with? You said you know him. What's his name?"

"Chief. They call him Chief."

"Is he a native?"

"I don't think so," Danny says. "I don't know where he's from. He used to come around the campground every so often, you know, bum a few smokes off me, scrounge for stuff the campers threw out in the Dumpster. There's a bunch of them out here. They have a little encampment. Seasonal workers, I guess."

"Seasonal workers? What kind of seasonal work?"

Danny watches her. One hand rests gently on the gun handle. She's very small, he thinks, now that she's outside of the truck. In her baggy uniform and braided fish and game visor cap, you almost couldn't tell if she were a man or a woman, he thinks. Except for those easy, sweet ripples of lemon-white hair.

"I don't know them," he says. "I don't know what they do for work or where they all came from. I just know they all live out here. They took over a spot where the Army had a little camp once or something. There's a trail that leads out of there, an old army road that cuts coastal out to the peninsula, I think." He pauses, suddenly realizing how odd it must sound that a body of people lives in the forest near him, apparently for no reason. "I don't know what they do all day."

"Except shoot bears in the head."

"Maybe it was self-defense?"

Fiona stops, turns halfway. They've just entered a small clearing. She squints into the dark canopy of branches to her right; nothing. Sunlight splashes everything—dead white logs, boulders, a thousand flying insects. She swats one away from her shimmering forehead. She turns and looks at Danny for the first time, which scares him further; her eyes are a deep lilac color and seem insane.

"He shot the bear, in the back of the head, close up," she says. "I examined the wound. It was like an execution."

Danny tries to picture the whole thing unfolding—maybe the bear is caught in a net, Chief approaching it from behind, arm extended, pistol in hand; other residents urging him on—but can't.

"I mean," Fiona continues. "You got to admit, that's pretty screwed up."

"Wow," Danny says. "That does sound pretty screwed up. I mean, why would anybody shoot a bear."

"I shot one once."

"Oh, uh, cool. Are you a hunter?"

"No. It was during my last day of training. I was bringing a nut hippie into camp, and I had the rifle. We ran straight up into a male griz standing over a fresh kill. We'd just crossed a wash, and there he was. Maybe twenty yards. We couldn't back out, and he started coming."

"Man," Danny says. "Training sucks."

"So the hippie I was with, he sat down and started singing to the bear. 'La, la, la.' In a real high voice like a bird or something."

"What did the bear do?"

"He did exactly what he was supposed to do."

"So what did you do?"

"I did exactly what I was supposed to do." Fiona takes a swig of water from an army surplus canteen she strapped to her holster, next to the revolver, and wipes her mouth with her sleeve, never taking her eyes from the dark patches of woods ahead of her. "I should have shot the hippie, not the bear. It wasn't the bear's fault. People are frigging idiots." She snaps the canteen back onto the holster. "Come on," she says. "Let's keep moving."

As they walk, Danny remembers his own training. Soon after the almost barroom brawl incident, Gretchen had driven him to an airport parking lot and dropped him off without saying a word—he had no idea what she was so angry about. From the airport he was sent up to an old logging camp for a week-long training and orientation. The bush pilot—who didn't say a word to him, look at him, or respond to him during the hour-long flight—handed him an envelope as soon as he was inside the plane containing a letter on forest service stationery informing him that he'd been assigned to a campground management position. The day was cold and clear, and a huge mass of mountains shined like a broken white refrigerator on the horizon, but all of Danny's hopeful adventure fantasies were destroyed. By the time the plane skimmed the lake surface and lurched up to the dock, Danny had sunk into the blackest of moods. He found his assigned cabin filled with trash and three bunks taken. He dumped the open luggage of his roommates off the fourth bunk, lay down, and stared up at the ceiling. A stocky young man in a sweatshirt suddenly burst through the door, chased by two matching partners, both of whom wore the same Greek letters on their T-shirts. The first picked up his pillow and threw it at the other two. They wrestled him to the ground and took turns goosing him while he giggled. Then he noticed Danny.

"Hey, bro?" the first one asked. "What's your name?"

"Danny."

"Danny what?"

Danny told them while pretending to read his manual.

"Well, from now on, bro," the first one declared, "you're Franny."

"Fine. I'm Franny." Danny really just wanted them to go away. Within three days of training, they did. The training was led by an ex-Marine who ran the cadets through the only kind of training he'd ever learned about. They set out each morning on marches across frozen mud, through tangled brush and vines, up and down steep ravines. The others complained about everything. "Screw this crap," one of them finally said. "I quit. Let's hit the coast, rent a boat, and do some fishing." Danny stayed and had his own cabin for the remainder of the training.

"We're getting close now," Danny says from some ten yards behind Fiona. He's still intently watching the hand on her gun.

The trail winds its way up over a small hill. The undergrowth opens up, and sunlight pours through large, gaping holes in the canopy. Twisting oak and maple trees mingle, then give way to a birch forest. Bark has been stripped from most of the trees, and the forest floor looks picked over. The trail breaks into a clearing. They enter the secret campground. Fiona slowly looks around at the ring of blue-tarp rectangular sheds, then walks straight toward two men standing by a smoldering fire. One of the men is tall and gaunt with a brown beard growing in patches. He wears an anorak and tattered hiking boots. The other man is short and dark with matted black hair and wears a black windbreaker with "Black Harbor Industries" stenciled on the back. Neither looks very happy to be approached by two people in uniform, one with a gun, who step suddenly out of the woods.

"Morning," Fiona says, walking straight up to them. They nod, then look back down into the red coals they've been warming their hands over. "Either of you tell me where I might find somebody who goes by the name of 'Chief'?"

"Who's looking for him?" the shorter man asks, his eyes moving from Fiona to Danny to Fiona's hand on the gun.

"Regional Fish and Game is looking for him," Fiona says. "Regional Fish and Game would like to ask him a few questions."

"May I ask what this is in reference to?" the tall one asks. The short one glares at him.

"In reference to? What are you, a frigging secretary?"

Their eyes swerve to a dark mass that crawls out from under a tarp tied to the face of a plywood shack that appears central and larger than the others. Danny recognizes Chief's bushy beard and the flat bald plate on the top of his head. In dirt-stained red long johns, Chief pulls his pants, boots, and hat out behind him. He struggles to get up; when he does, he is surprised to see the newcomers. Instantly, he pulls the hat onto his head.

"Is this Chief?" Fiona asks.

"No," the short one says. "That ain't him."

"Hey, Chief," the taller one says. "This lady would like a word with you."

"Oh, yeah?" Chief says. "Does she mind if I hitch up my trousers first?"

"We understand that you are in possession of a firearm, a handgun," Fiona says.

"So are you."

"Is the gun in your shed?"

"Shed?" Chief looks to Short and Tall. "This ain't a shed. This here's my double-wide."

"I need you to bring me the gun," Fiona says.

"I ain't going to bring you no gun."

"I said I need you to bring me the gun."

"Chief," Danny says, "Come on now."

"You told her I got a gun?"

Danny looks at the others. "No," Danny says.

"Well, this is a free country, screw all," Chief says. "This is my homestead. These people are my guests. And you ain't invited on my property."

"This is government property," Fiona says. "If we need to evict you, we will. And if we need to arrest you, we will."

They stand six feet apart. Fiona glares at Chief, who appears to inflate himself to a much larger size. He looks around at the campsite—the horseshoe of little shacks and tents—possibly hoping, Danny thinks, that his loyalists will rise up and rush her. Danny can detect people rustling around in their shelters, half-awake, but not coming out, sensing that some kind of micro-disaster is coming down.

"Was it you?" Chief says again to Danny. "Did you tell her I have a gun?"

"You need to bring me the gun," Fiona says.

"Sorry," Chief smiles at Fiona. "I guess you're going to have to arrest me."

"Come with me," Fiona says. She removes her hand from her revolver and reaches for a pair of handcuffs. She steps toward Chief, who towers over her. Danny and the others freeze.

Chief looks at her, stunned. Suddenly he yelps. "No!" he screams, slapping at her hand as she reaches for his arm. His legs buckle, and he falls flat on his back. Tears squirt out of the corners of his eyes. "I'm not going!" he yells. "I'm not go-ing!"

Fiona stands over him, reaching down to pin him to the ground with her free hand, but is unable to get a grip on him. She looks to Danny for a second.

Chief suddenly squirts out from under her and lunges for the woods, like a wounded animal. He throws himself into the brush, which closes around him, and disappears. A log crashes somewhere in the distance, then the woods are si-lent.

Fiona, who has pulled out her gun but holds it to her hip, stares into the woods after Chief. Then she turns to Danny.

"Thanks so much, ranger," she says. "You've been a great help."

FEBRUARY 1942

Crunch leads
the way

This is a dry inland snow, Rodney tells himself, watching the first glassy sparkles brush against his padded sleeves. Rodney stops and leans against his axe handle. He pauses only long enough to take measure of the gray swirl bearing down on him from the brighter clouds. This is not the wet ocean snow that drags its icy fingers through the core of men stuck sweating through it, rattling their bare ribs, weighing them down. This snow smells different. It has a different weight and bearing. The ocean snow smells more salty, dense, and menacing. Ocean snow is a bad snow, but this is a dry snow, Rodney thinks, picking up the axe and slowly swinging it into the meat of the branch before him. This is a good snow.

"Coming *at* you!"

In the gray dim ahead, Rodney can make out a rope stringing itself taught, pulling and then bending a giant of a fir tree. The branches, crusted in ice, shiver out a cloud of snow, needles, sticks before it all crashes into the frozen earth. The air fills with a smell like Pine-Sol or a giant menthol cigarette. Around the fallen tree, three shrouded figures work in unison to extricate the rope. Even in the thin winter light, Rodney can easily make out Crunch, a full head above the others and twice as wide, already looking to the next tree blocking their path.

"Next *tree!*"

Crunch is already hacking at the base. One of the two other figures scrambles up the branches to set the ropes.

Rodney and the three figures around him swing their axes harder, still clearing what they guess might be a roadway to what they guess might be a front line or a beachhead or a way out of this frozen entanglement. For now, they have one more tree. One more tree, one more tree before another black night swallows them whole.

The first miracle happened eight days after they were sent blindly into the snowy wilderness. With two small sleds piled with saws, axes, ropes, shovels, box rations, and thin blankets—and with a promise from a shivering lieutenant that crates of winter boots, parkas, gloves, winter tents, and hot food were right behind them—a detachment of twenty-five soldiers, including Rodney and Crunch, began shoveling and chopping a path through the forest. At nightfall, they huddled together under the blankets while a snowstorm raged around them. In the morning, the lieutenant and half of their colleagues were nowhere to be seen. Even worse, the path they had just cleared was buried in snow.

"Should we go back?" Rodney asked Crunch through chattering teeth.

"Hell no," Crunch said. "We go back, and we disobey orders. We disobey, man. Don't you see? We're already penal. We go back there now, and there's no telling. We have to move forward, friend. They want a road, so we need to build them a road."

For two weeks they chopped their way deeper and deeper into the forest, following the contours of one mountain ridge and then another. The surrounding trees protected them, it seemed, from the worst of the wind and the cold. But each day, with rations dwindling and the cold getting worse, Rodney fell further into weakness and despair. Each morning another soldier disappeared, trying to find his way back or just giving up altogether.

"We're gonna die out here for sure," somebody chattered one morning as they attempted to unfold themselves from the blankets and bodies.

"I'd rather die out here than die back there," Crunch said. "Out here I'll die doing my duty. I'd rather die out here than die in a soldier's prison. You want to shiver, man? The memory of that prison is what makes me shiver."

That morning their luck turned. A giant shadow passed through the thin strands of light filtering through the trees. A roaring noise swept through the forest, followed by a thick, hollow thud somewhere just over the next ridge.

They followed the smell of smoke. There wasn't a lot left of the airplane, but scattered about the wreckage in the snow were shattered wooden crates filled with hundreds of par-kas, snow pants, lined boots, snowshoes, tents, crates filled with canned foods, fuel canisters, heaters, ropes, brand-new saws and axes, gloves, hats, and rifles—a crate full of rifles with ammunition. Nobody had survived the crash. There were no signs of a pilot or crew. The fuselage was in flames. Rodney and Crunch and the last five soldiers of the detach-ment stood as close to the flames as they could—stripping off their tattered rags, standing on crates in their under-pants, skeletons; even the giant Crunch stood on stick legs, ribs sticking out, soaking up the great heat. When the fire faded, they climbed into their new winter gear, piled their sleds with the new supplies, and returned to their work.

With no instructions, no directions, and no map—but much better equipped, warmer, and safer from the ele-ments—the remaining crew members worked in shifts, in-stinctively following the contours of the mountain scape and following the direction they thought the lieutenant pointed them in two, then three, then four weeks before. The seven remaining men grew stronger. They had a singular purpose: axes and saws, axes and saws, into the next wall of trees, the next wall of snow. Something resembling a road snaked back behind them, but the forest seemed to close behind them. Bulldozers were supposed to follow, but they never heard any machinery. On occasion they heard airplanes above the clouds and distant thunder that could be artillery or could be weather. The sun started shining through the endless wall of winter clouds.

Four weeks in, just when they started to convince themselves that the cruelest months of winter might be behind them, a big storm hit at night with such intensity that it shredded the tents and pelted them with hail the size of baseballs. They dug themselves out and looked back on the pathway they had cleared, now filled with fallen, shattered trees and snowdrifts. Then they retrieved all the gear and equipment they could find and set themselves back to work, moving forward, ever forward.

"What do you say we scout this out?" Crunch says to Rodney at the end of this, their forty-second day in the wilderness. The day's light is dimming. They are both leaning on their axe handles.

"Getting late," Rodney says, but he knows better than to protest. "Let's be quick about it."

The other men march back to the snow cave they built, sealed with the shredded remains of the tents, to get a fire started. Rodney waves to them as they descend the freshly cleared path, but they don't see him in the diminishing light. Rodney watches them disappear into the woods, shrouded gray figures moving in the murky snow-forest. *I don't even know their names,* Rodney thinks. *I have to learn their names.* Then he turns to follow Crunch into the dense tangle of trees ahead.

Marching through the entanglement in their snowshoes, fully encased in the branches above, it is impossible to tell how much time has passed. "Check this out," Crunch yells ahead. Rodney follows him into an open area. It is almost fully dark now. As his eyes adjust, he sees that they are standing in a bowl, a ridgeline ahead of them, and beyond that a wall of clouds forming quickly, as if they are being pushed up from something far below. Big, wet flakes start floating around them.

"We should turn back now," Rodney says.

"Just a second now," Crunch says. "I just need to see what's over that lip over there."

Rodney follows Crunch into a sudden blow of damp wind, then a fierce blast of snow. The wind presses them both down. Rodney tries to follow Crunch's outline, then his snowshoe tracks. He tries hollering, but the wind eats his voice. He has to keep moving. He pushes onward and onward, and then his legs disappear beneath him. He has stepped over a ledge, and he is flying. He is flying straight down into a giant crevasse. How stupid is this, Rodney thinks. After all this. This is so stupid of me. He waits for the inevitable impact, the end of all this suffering. He pictures his mom, his little brother, Crunch, the five soldiers whose names he never learned all staring down at him from the top of the ledge, watching him fall, waiting for him to crash. But the crash never happens. It is like he is cupped in a soft, giant mitten. It is the snow that I thought would kill me, Rodney thinks before falling unconscious. It is the snow, in the end, that will save me.

Rodney wakes up to something familiar wafting through the air—the smell of frying fish. He sits up, brushes the snow from his parka, and looks over to where Crunch lies flat on his back, half-buried in snow and snoring. Rodney crawls over and shakes him awake. They stare up at a huge cliff, hundreds of feet above them. Rodney points down to a lone gulley that they fell into, sliding down a sheet of ice into this mountain of snow.

"I guess we got lucky again," Rodney says.

"No way in hell we're climbing back up there," Crunch says.

They follow the smell down into the woods, where it grows stronger. They burst through a clump of brush and almost trip over an old man in the snow, sitting by a fire, roasting fish on sticks. Instinctively Rodney and Crunch put their hands up. The old man puts his hands up. All three burst into laughter. The old man hands each of them a fish on a stick. Rodney asks how they can climb back up the cliff.

"You probably can't," he says. "It is like a great mountain that split in half." It goes for miles in both directions. In broken English, the man, wrapped in a gray parka with a fur-lined hood, explains to them that this stretch of land has been his family's traditional winter home for generations, but something has happened to the place, with strange men and machines. The man gestures to the sky.

"All of my family has left, and I am following them. Something bad is here now. This place has gone crazy."

He tells them of a settlement a few days' walk along the seacoast. "I do not know who lives there, if anybody," he says. "You'll want to be careful." The old man points them toward the sea. They thank him and set out for the settlement.

"Maybe we should follow the old man out?" Rodney says.

"No way in hell, man," Crunch says. "We are now, officially, deserters. You do what you want to, but me? I'm taking my chances with the settlement. Can't be worse than what's waiting for us back there."

AUGUST 1983

FROM *THE ONLY PLANET GUIDE:* THE GREAT GULF WILDERNESS

While the name "Great Gulf" is intended specifically for a natural 5,000-foot-deep cut between two split mountain ranges crossing the peninsula, the three hundred–mile sweep of land between Portia and this fault line is often referred to as the Great Gulf Wilderness. Bordered by the towering coastal mountain ranges to the west and east, the Great Gulf Wilderness is defined by deep, tangled, and somewhat impenetrable forest. The Old Soldier's Highway, snaking through this maze of massive trees, raging rivers, boulders, and ledges, is actually the culmination of a number of roads cut through the forest, some intentionally and others mistakenly, during the Great Panic. The highway (actually a two-lane gravel-and-mud road) is dotted with occasional clusters of general stores, diners, gas stations, and log cabins. Camping is often accomplished simply by pulling over on the side of the road. In recent years, lodgings for travelers have sprung up; the few of these that have been successful have done so by taking weeklong reservations months in advance, and by building their own airstrips and flying visitors in directly from Petrolia Airport to the north. The owners of these lodges often seek to discourage visits from "transients," and travelers headed upland are wiser to keep moving.

Two hundred miles up, the Old Soldier's Highway splits in two directions at the settlement of Cabbage, a bustling, lawless little settlement with a few bars, diners, and motels among auto repair stores (always a brisk business), hunter supplies, etc. To the left, a forest service road travels another *thirty-eight miles to the Great Gulf Wilderness Regional Park; to the right, the highway continues another hundred miles, north by northeast, to the City of Petrolia.*

Great Gulf Wilderness Regional Park, established in 1978, seeks to preserve one of the peninsula's most spectacular natural sites. The Great Gulf itself is a narrow, straight chasm between sheer cliffs, following a fault line that cuts across the peninsula. Rolling, 5,000- to 6,000-foot mountains rise up quickly from the valley floor, pushing up against one another before tumbling into the craggy western coast. Thunderstorms, dense fog, and summer blizzards rise without warning from the ocean, stripping the higher elevations of plant life. It is a barren and spectacular place, especially when the sun breaks through, which is quite rare. The regional forest service has established a park headquarters at the park gate where backpackers can register for campsites. A backcountry campground has been established, a three-mile hike up a well-maintained side trail that connects with the twenty-six–mile Gulf Trail. The clearly marked Gulf Trail ascends another five miles beyond the campground to Gulf Mountain, the highest point in the park and a spectacular view on those days when there is any view at all. From Gulf Mountain it is easy to see why further exploration and settlement has proven elusive. On the other side of the gulf, even larger, more precipitous peaks climb into the sky, seemingly endlessly. At the park headquarters, more robust wilderness explorers can secure backcountry permits to explore off trail and on foot, although this is discouraged for all but the most experienced travelers. Bear canisters are provided.

A final note: From the Gulf Trail and throughout the park, old trails and logging roads fan out in all directions. Explorers of these paths have described markings of old encampments, army vehicles, and other wreckage of Grizzle's past. Conservationists have discussed reclaiming these trails, possible linking the Great Gulf back to Portia; but in the meantime, hikers are discouraged from exploring unmarked trails.

Chief slides down
the snowpack

Chief slides down the steep, dirty snowpack between two stone ledges alone. His backpack is top-heavy and almost throws him at every switchback. The ledges are shrouded in vapor; dark gullets of rainwater wash down the slippery rocks beneath his boots. To Chief it doesn't matter. Nothing matters, so long as he gets down below tree line where he will be safe from three days and nights of wind and rain.

At the base of the ledges, his trail re-enters the forest. A small brown sign with white letters points north, announcing he has now linked paths with the main trail, which follows the valley floor into government parkland. In six miles the trail enters a backcountry campsite, then it climbs to the highest summit in the range, now safely obscured from view, some eleven miles ahead. Beyond the summit lies the gulf, a jagged chasm slicing through the mountain range. At the bottom is the trail his old friend Hawk told him about that will lead him to Grizzletown.

After last night's rainstorm, and despite the loss of altitude that will have to be regained, Chief's glad to get back to the low trail. Safe now, under a dense canopy of trees, Chief sits down on a log. He drinks from a bottle and wipes his head. He looks back up at the rocky ledges he's just descended from and follows the gray outline ahead. Chief thinks of the campground. Maybe I can scrounge some food there, he thinks. Then he thinks of the trouble he's in—they'll be looking for me. He pictures an army of backcountry rangers with bloodhounds, scouring the wilderness.

The trail follows a hissing brook. At noon, Chief crosses another side trail. The sign references a road, just 2.1 miles down. He considers packing down and trying to hitch a ride but thinks better of it. He's bushwhacked, crossing slippery snowfields and sleeping under a tarp in the cold rain for three nights. Now he finds the trail gentle and the sunlight, shining from a blue sky above the treetops, comforting. Then the trail starts climbing again.

It is only a week since Chief's confrontation with the rangers. That night he snuck back into the Portia encampment, gathered his belongings in his backpack, and snuck out without anyone seeing him. Now, sweating under the weight of his pack, Chief comes to a footbridge crossing a steep, violent gush of water. On the far side of the bridge, a woman stoops under an oversized backpack, one hand on one knee. She looks sternly at a little boy in a baseball cap, staring sternly at a daypack lying on the ground. They are the first people he's seen since leaving the secret campground. Chief crosses the bridge. Passing them, trying not to breathe too hard, he lifts an arm and waves.

"Hello!" the woman says cheerfully.

"Howdy," Chief mumbles.

"My backpack's broken," the boy says.

"Oh yeah?" Chief tries to step around the boy, who misinterprets the gesture and hands him his pack.

Chief's hands shudder as he pulls on a few straps and quickly hands it back to the boy.

"I fixed it," Chief says.

"I don't think so," the boy replies as he puts the pack down on a rock.

"Thanks anyway," his mother laughs as Chief hurries away.

*

The trail opens to tent sites clustered around a small alpine lake. Chief stops and circles the campground through the woods. He sets his pack in a grove of white birch trees, framed by the granite walls of a huge crevasse. He struggles to string up his tattered blue tarp between two trunks. He lays down on his musty, moth-eaten sleeping bag and pulls his sweat-soaked, broad-brimmed hat down over his eyes. He can smell food cooking from camp stoves; through the woods he can barely make out smoke trailing from a few occupied sites. It's getting late in the season, he knows; most of the backcountry campers headed back downland weeks ago. It's getting cold up here in the higher elevations, Chief chuckles to himself. It's way too cold for the backpacky downlanders. The smoke shifts and blows into the birch grove. Someone's cooking something good, Chief measures with his nostrils. It's a beef stroganoff or a tuna alfredo. He pulls his second and final bottle of cheap, generic whiskey from his pack and takes a long pull, waiting for the whiskey to warm his fingers. When his fingers are warm, he rolls over and gets up, picks up his water bottle and flashlight, and strides with authority into the center of the campground.

At the center of a ring of sites, there's a spigot; he walks straight up to it and fills the water bottle. When he turns around, he's startled to see the woman he saw earlier, the one with the child, sitting alone at a picnic table. Pieces of a camp stove lie on the table before her. Strands of bright brass-colored hair poke out in all directions. She looks up and smiles.

"Hey! You know how to put one off these things together?"

"No, not really. Sorry."

She shrugs, then looks back down at the stove.

He starts to leave, but the whiskey kicks in. "Well, actually, let me see that," Chief says. He sits down across from her. He picks up a piece that looks like a nozzle and screws it into a piece that looks like a faucet. "I think this goes here," he says. He attaches the faucet to a piece that looks like a spark plug, then stands it up. When he lets go, it falls down.

"I guess the proper answer is no," he says. "I guess I don't know how to put one of these things together."

"Oh well," she says. "It doesn't matter, I've got my old one in my pack."

"Where's your little buddy?"

"Who, Jack? He's taking a nap back at the lean-to over there. He's a little beat."

"That's a pretty steep climb."

"Yeah, well, we couldn't just set up camp right there. I was pretty nice about it."

"Yeah, well." Obviously nothing's going on with dinner here, Chief thinks; he glances around quickly but doesn't see other campers. I'll have to sneak down later, he thinks. "Sorry about your stove," he says, getting up from the table.

"Hey, you want to come back and have a cup of hot chocolate with us? I'm sure Jack's waking up by now. I think he was a little captivated by you back there, that's all. I think he'd get a kick out of talking to you."

"Sounds great."

"Unless you're some kind of escaped fugitive or something."

"No," Chief says. "No, I'm not."

"Glad to hear it," she says.

Jack wakes up as they arrive, just as the first stars pop into the sky. "Hello, Jack," she says.

"Hello." He rotates his head in the sleeping bag. He reaches one arm out for his baseball cap and pulls it tightly over his head. He pulls the bag up around his neck like a turtle.

"I found your pal here, the backpack repairman, wandering around," she says. "Only I didn't catch his name. What's your name?"

"Um, they call me, um, Tony," Chief says.

"Oh. They call me Sara."

She reaches into her pack, perched on a corner post, and pulls out a small nylon bag. "That's Jack." She screws an old stove together. "This'll just take a minute." She hooks the stove to a fuel canister, primes it, and lights it. An orange flame leaps into the air, then tunes down to a steady blue hiss. She places a pot on top, fills it with water, and puts on a lid.

Jack leaps out of his sleeping bag and gathers the water bottle and the nylon bag together neatly by the stove. Then he scurries to pick up two aluminum hot chocolate wrappers that Sara has absentmindedly dropped. She stirs the hot chocolate, then pours it into two cups and a tin bowl. She hands Chief the bowl. "Here, you're bigger. You get the bowl." The hot chocolate warms him, differently. The moon starts to rise above the next range.

"It's so peaceful here," Sarah says. "How long have you been out here?"

"Been a while now."

"Do you get scared?" Jack asks.

"No." Chief picks up the bowl again. "Nothing scares me."

"I don't like storms," Jack says.

"Yeah, they get pretty fierce up here in the backcountry," Chief says matter-of-factly, sucking hot chocolate through his teeth until they hurt. "Man's got to be prepared for whatever it is Old Mother Wilderness's going to throw at him."

"I like hot chocolate," Jack says. "I like hot chocolate and breakfast and airplanes."

"Well, I best be moving on," Chief says. "Up with the sun. Before the weather sets in."

"Oh, sure!" Sara says. "Sorry to keep you so long."

"Thanks for the hot chocolate."

"Sure! Say goodbye, Jack."

Jack takes the bowl from Chief and places it neatly underneath his cup. "Goodbye," he says.

"Well, goodbye," Chief says. He walks back toward the woods, scanning the trees for where the other campers have bear-hung their food supplies.

Chief wakes up cursing, curled in a ball under his tarp. The sun has risen over the far ridge. It's much later than he intended. He hastily ropes the tarp together, stuffs the items he grabbed last night—a bag of food, a fuel canister, a fleece hooded pullover—into his bag, on top of his more valued items, and laces up his boots. What I really need is a stove, he tells himself. A stove so I don't make smoke. He longingly thinks of Sara's stove for a second, then erases the thought. He decided he wasn't going to rip off Sara because she'd been nice to him, and he'd developed a soft spot for the kid. He'd thought about this, lying curled up under his tarp the night before, sipping a few last sips to help him forget where he was, and that there was more backcountry ahead of him, three or four days, before he was across the park and to the road.

It takes another hour for Chief to circle the outskirts of the campsite and locate the trail again. Once on it, he knows if he keeps his eyes out, he can avoid other hikers and make it to the gulf by noon. If he can cross the gulf by nightfall, he can disappear into the bush. The trail is exposed, in a glacial bowl climbing above tree line, but for the moment it is the only way to get where he's going. He sets out so sure of his ability to scout out the trail ahead of him that when he turns a corner around a boulder and runs straight into Sara and Jack sitting on a rock sharing an apple, he almost bursts out laughing.

"Hey, Tony!" Sara says, "We decided to make a go of it, just hike up to the glacier. I just want to show Jack what a glacier's like. Are you heading up that way? Would we hold you up if we walked with you for a spell?"

"Great," Chief says, looking back over his shoulder. Perfect cover until he gets to the gulf. "No problem at all."

They climb up a set of stone steps and pass around the pond. The glacier leans against the mountainside. Sara leads Chief on the trail, shooing Jack ahead with one hand. She stops and smiles at the rock walls next to her. "Look, Jack, check it out."

"What?" Jack smiles. Sara's hands run across the brittle rock outcropping. "Quartzite."

Jack's hands follow hers. "Yeah," he says.

"Check it out Jack, look," Sara says, pointing up. "A barn swallow. Check out how he follows the ledge so close. He's looking for something." Chief looks at blue and yellow sparkles in the high grass growing between the rocks.

"Check out these flowers," he says.

"Wow, yeah, check them out Jack." The gulf opens around them. A chute of freezing water sprays them as it cascades down the snowpack. The trail turns into steps carved into the rock, winding up the cliff. Jack charges ahead, climbing the steps with great strides, then stops and waits for them to pass. They cross a ledge blackened by spillover water. Chief reaches a hand back for Jack. "Well, I guess we'll follow you up just a little farther," Sara says. "Maybe just up to the top of the ridge. If that's all right."

At the top of the ridge, Jack sits down on a rock. They are pressed against a slope of boulders. The slopes reach out like long arms on either side of them before plunging down into the gulf below. Stacked cairns mark a path up to a high ledge, somewhere just over the rim. Great white clouds jostle for position above them.

"What do you say, Jack?" Sara asks him. "You want to push on a little farther?"

"I got a rock in my shoe," Jack replies. He struggles to pull a white sneaker off one foot, then the other.

"That's some rock," Sara says.

"It's not so far now," Chief says, taking stock of the clouds.

"Come on, Jack. You want to go for it?" Sara asks him. "It's just over that hill there, really. There's a big rock outcropping, we can see the whole world. We can split a Hershey bar." Sara reaches down to pick up his shoes and tie them back on his feet.

The wind is colder and stronger at the edge of the gulf. Chief looks down into the abyss below and panics. I've got to find a way down this, he thinks, reaching instinctively to make sure his last bottle is still in his bag. They climb under a short ledge and pull their hoods around their heads. A wall of darker, heavier clouds reaches up at them from the far side of the mountain.

"That's some view," Sara says. Chief's thoughts have drifted back to the wilderness warning posters he once saw in a ranger station. Photos of shrouded bodies huddled together. A rescue team in orange raingear walking a stretcher down a trail. Clouds engulf them. Chief can no longer see his feet sticking out in front of him. The air is wet. Huge drops of water form on their raincoats.

Then, just as suddenly, the cloud detaches itself. They watch it climb up to the sky. Sitting between them, Jack takes one last bite of the chocolate bar. His eyes roll up into the back of his head, and he slides gently down to his mother's lap. A bigger, darker wall of clouds lurches toward them. A rumbling echo, of thunder or a plane or sliding rocks, echoes off the next ridge.

"The weather's not looking so good," Chief says. "I best move on."

"Yeah," Sara says, stroking Jack's hair. "I better not let him fall asleep." But she does; in seconds his mouth falls open.

"Maybe I can carry him down piggyback," she says. "Do you think you can carry both packs? At least for a spell, until we're off of this ledge."

"I guess," Chief says.

"I think there's another trail back to the campsite. It follows the ledge for a bit, then circles back to the campsite. If you can just help me find it. I don't know if you're headed in that direction."

Chief picks up her backpack and pulls it on his back next to his own; if he leans forward for a bit, he thinks he can manage. "We better go for it," he says.

"Yeah, then," Sara says. A new cloud sucks them in. "I guess we should make a run for it."

"So it's an international school, where I'm going to be teaching in the fall. It's overseas."

Sara, two feet in front of Chief, disappears and then reappears, testing the next slate shelf with her foot. Jack is slumped across her shoulders. Chief can hardly see or hear her. They've been stumbling in thick fog for almost an hour, climbing down a series of granite shelves, searching for trail markings. The rumbles occur infrequently, keeping a safe distance for the moment. The wind grows fierce. It's getting colder. Chief is sagging under the weight of the packs, pressing down against his lower spine. A pool of warm sweat has formed between Chief's back, his poncho, and the packs. If they stop, the warmth will evaporate. He leans forward to keep the weight centered, trying not to tumble into the darkness.

"Yeah," Sara yells over the wind. "Hey! Here's a marker, I think. That's another cairn up ahead, I think. So there's students from all over the world there. Jack's going to be in the first grade with kids from all over. Yeah. I couldn't imagine putting him in a better environment." Sara stops and surveys the gray mass ahead of them. "Do you think we're lost?"

"Don't think so," Chief says. He thinks of the people he read about when he was downland, the people who went to Grizzle and how they died—hypothermia, slipping on ice, summer blizzards, walking off ledges. A family of four, exposed, found a few summers before, was beaten to death by hail. He watches Sara slip on a ledge, then right herself. He could leave them up here, he thinks. It's not Chief's fault; he certainly didn't make them come up here.

"Do you think we should turn back, go back for the trail we came up?"

"No," Chief says. "We're down too far now."

Her calm tone feeds his urgency. They're slowing him down, Chief thinks. It crosses his mind that the first spot that looks like it leads safely down into the gulf he should just make a run for it. Chief looks down at a cold black puddle between two slabs of rock. It's frozen solid. His throat is dry; he licks the icy water collecting on his lips. The wind shifts; a spray of stinging mist slaps his face. Another rumble, closer this time, seems to surround them.

"Well, I guess we should push on," Sara says. "Try to find another marker, huh." The fog grows several degrees darker, like night is falling. A chill passes through Chief. His nylon poncho flaps wildly in the wind. Jack tucks his little hands into Sara's shirt around her neck, seeming to choke her. Somehow he's still sleeping. Chief can see him shudder.

I wouldn't be the first, Chief thinks. It wouldn't be my fault.

"Here's one! Here's one, I think." Sara points ahead to one rock sitting atop another. "Do you think it's a cairn?" It clearly isn't. White light briefly illuminates the fog, a yellow-brown, then darker. A breath later, a clear crack of thunder rattles over his shoulder, just over the summits behind them. "We're almost down now," she says, wiping water off of her face. Her hood has blown off her head. Her hair is soaked and wild. "Man, I'm glad we met you though. We'd be pretty screwed if you weren't here."

Another crack. Closer this time. Chief is sure he feels a charge pass through him. Jack loses his grip; he slides slowly down Sara's back. His eyes are sealed; his face, tucked in where the drawstring pulls the hood close to the skin, is white. Sara slides him down onto a stone shelf, and kneels to hold him there; as she does Chief takes three steps back. Sara looks at Chief, first with confusion, then with a wave of fear, as he starts stepping away.

"You're not going to leave us up here?"

The cloud wraps around her quickly, like a thick cape, and he is off, stumbling down the ledges, faster now. He runs right into a sign pointing to the right, to the campsite, just two miles away. An opening appears on the left, a goat trail or something plunging down into the abyss. Chief falls down repeatedly, sliding on his backside, all the way down.

A mile down, or two, the cloud lifts. Chief stands on a lunar landscape, one sharp granite rock pressed up against another, in the bottom of a huge ravine. Spread out before him, yellow beams of sunlight heat the valley floor, rise up the face of the next ridge, and stop abruptly on ripped ribbons of cloud hanging in purple and black just above his head. A last gasp of thunder drifts away, quieter now, against the next ridge.

Chief stands there for just a second, licking the cold water dripping down his face. He had no idea how thirsty he's become. He reaches for his bottle. That's when he realizes that Sara's backpack—with two camping stoves, food, and sleeping bags—is still hanging over his left shoulder, and his backpack is hanging on his right. Maybe there's meds in there, Chief thinks. Maybe she's got anxiety meds. Maybe the kid's got something. They'll be okay, he thinks. They'll find the sign;

they have no idea how close they are. He points himself north, and soon a new trail opens up in the valley before him.

FROM *THE ONLY PLANET GUIDE*: PETROLIA AND ITS SURROUNDINGS

For those who have made the long trip all the way up from Portia and beyond on the Old Soldier's Highway, logging so many miles of pristine wilderness travel: Brace yourselves. Soon after you leave Cabbage, you will begin to see signs of brand-new, horrifying, unregulated development. The strip that winds from Cabbage down into the valley that houses the port city of Petrolia, Grizzle's largest and fastest growing settlement, is a shock. Clearings along the highway have been deforested to accommodate businesses seeking to prosper from new visitors flooding in from the airport. Inflatable gorillas and lumberjacks float above the trees, selling fireworks and hunting supplies. Bars and liquor stores are frequent, as are multiservice general store/gas stations and roadside motels. Trailer parks have popped up alongside many of the most beautiful lakeside spots to house a surging seasonal working population— fast-food workers, housekeepers, waitresses, and gas station attendants—all shipped in from the mainland (and in many cases from overseas, with no knowledge of where they would be working). Nobody seems happy here, and very few stay for long.

One brief reprieve from the madness is the Regional Fish and Game headquarters, a squat military building where fishing and hunting permits are issued, and rangers offer backcountry guidance to travelers. Please note that, for those planning on hunting, fishing, and trapping in the wilderness, permits are required, and laws are strictly enforced. Penalties are steep for poachers or others who decide to forgo the law. Each year, Fish and Game posts a listing of seasonal dates for sportsman.

Passing through this chaos, one finally enters Petrolia, a vast entanglement of new urban sprawl circling a wide harbor ringed with smoking oil refineries. The city is lined with bars, flophouses (converted from barracks), and hastily assembled apartment complexes housing oil refinery workers, sailors, military personnel, and loggers. There is a hospital, a jail, and the airport (on occasion, discouraged travelers have been known to ditch their cars and buy one-way plane tickets home, ending their Grizzle adventure in Petrolia). Many of the fish and game, forest service, and other administrators operate from Petrolia, including the busy helicopter and boat rescue crews who constantly circle the peninsula searching for lost travelers. Between this population, the oft-embittered seasonal worker population, and travelers who have flown in for recreational purposes, the town has a Wild West feel to it. Again, for travelers on a budget who seek a wilderness experience, it is best to resupply in Petrolia, fill up on gas, and keep moving. The mountains encircling the city offer endless opportunities to pull over and camp by a glacial creek or a mountain lake (one that, preferably, does not have a trailer park on its shores).

For most travelers, Black Harbor, thirty miles north of Petrolia, is the official end of the road. A small settlement encircling a beautiful body of water where glacial ice meets the ocean, Black Harbor has recently hosted an August event, the Black Harbor Music Festival, where the few musicians who play the peninsula's bars come to perform before an audience that camps in the woods around a stage. Local small farms that grow spectacularly oversized produce show and sell vegetables and berries under a pavilion (a great opportunity for travelers to stock up on healthy greens). Local authorities have sought to close down the festival, claiming that it attracts the wrong element. Beyond Black Harbor, the road winds another ten miles toward the eastern stretch of the Great Gulf and an unnamed volcano that towers above the harbor. The volcano, never completely dormant, erupted in 1972, closing off a small military road leading to outer Grizzle and the rumored settlement of Grizzletown. The road officially ends at this point, and foot traffic beyond this point is discouraged.

Eva brings her earrings
to the festival

In the laundromat, Eva reads a posted sign advertising the Great North Star Music Fair, on this day, thirty miles north. As Eva tells her idea to Ernie, her voice races. Eventually he looks up from the classifieds.

"I've strung twelve pairs of earrings," she says. "I'll sell them at the exit gate for twenty bucks apiece. It's a folk festival. I know I can sell them at a folk festival."

"But it's today," Ernie says. "You think it'll work?"

Eva frowns. "I think I know my market."

In the parking lot, they sit on the hatchback bumper. Ernie leans against their gear, finishing a six-pack, still circling job listings. Eva painstakingly paints the word "inspirations" in silver across the front of a purple shoebox. She carefully places the twelve pairs of delicate blue and pink and purple beaded earrings in the box. Ernie closes the hatch, and Eva turns the key. The engine coughs, then stops breathing.

"I'll check the fan belt," Ernie says.

"It's not the fan belt."

Ernie lifts the hood and stares down at the engine. "Well, it's not the fan belt." He jiggles the wires. "Maybe it's the water pump again. Try it again."

Eva leans on the wheel, immersing it in tangles of hair. Ernie goes back to the trunk and pulls out the gear. She picks up the box of earrings and follows.

*

At four o'clock, Eva and Ernie get a ride in the back of a brown truck. The driver hands two dripping cans of Coors through the sliding cab window.

"Thanks!" Ernie yells. He offers a can to Eva, pinned between their backpacks and a panting wet dog who smells like fish. In her lap she holds the box, the little earrings nestled like eggs. She stares at the beer. Ernie pulls it away. He slurps the first can down and opens the second.

"How far you going?" the driver yells.

"To the end of the road," Ernie yells back.

"Yeah? You going to that music fair?"

"Planning on it."

"It's over at five sharp. Sheriff's orders. He's a hard ass. You know that?"

"Yeah, I know."

"He's not a real sheriff, by the way. They just think he is. Where you hitch up from?"

"Back there. Car died."

"Man. Alternator?"

"Yeah, maybe." Ernie shrugs. "Maybe the water pump."

Eva focuses on untwisting her hair. The dog licks her bare arm. It turns to Ernie, its tongue hanging out.

"Hey," the driver yells. "You want a couple more beers?"

It's five o'clock. Ernie and Eva walk up a dirt road. The sky darkens. It smells like rain. The earrings shuffle in the box.

"Yo, bear," Ernie calls into the woods. "Nice bear."

They enter a clearing. Men lean on trucks.

"How you doing?" Ernie says.

A red-faced man in a bear-claw necklace, a gold badge pinned to a sheepskin coat, glares at Ernie. Eva freezes, gripping the shoebox.

"The fair up this way?"

"You're a little late, young man. Fair's over."

"Problem here, sheriff?" another yells.

"No problem here," the sheriff answers. "These folks here were just headed home."

"Yes, sir," Ernie says. "Just headed home."

They sit on their packs on a highway ramp. It rains, then blows over. The luminous evening sky turns the highway puddles silver. Just beyond the trees, clouds lift, revealing rows of jagged blue mountains. Eva turns to Ernie to see if he's watching. He's staring across the road at a bar called Smokey's. Each window flashes a different neon beer sign.

It's nine o'clock in Smokey's. Two thick-bearded men sit across from Eva and Ernie with a huge, sweating, fresh pitcher of beer.

One of the men points to their backpacks. "So, are you hikers or something?"

"Yeah," Ernie says. "We're gonna do some backcountry."

"Backcountry?" He snorts. "Up here we call it *bear* country. You got a gun?"

"Nah, nothing like that."

Eva stares across the room at two women at a table.

"How about pepper spray. You got pepper spray?"

Ernie tilts his pitcher. The beer pours from its side, in a wide arc, into his glass.

"We know what we're doing."

"Man. Couldn't catch me out there dead."

"Those two women look so nice," Eva whispers. Ernie looks over. They wear nice rain parkas. They're eating salads and laughing. Their hair is long and clean and straight. "Look at their eyes," Eva whispers, then she looks at her box.

"They, like, match these blue bead earrings. This is perfect." Eva grips the box, then starts to get up.

One of the men squints at the smudged paint on the crumpled box.

"What's a 'spirater'?"

"Inspirations," Ernie says.

"They're earrings," Eva says. "I make earrings."

"Oh. You want another pitcher? On us?"

The two women get up to leave. Eva watches them go, then stares down at her box.

"Sounds great," Ernie says. "Thanks!"

It's midnight. Eva follows Ernie up a muddy trail. Someone in the bar told them there was a terrific free campsite, full of seasonal workers, up one of these trails.

"Yo, bear," Ernie calls into the thicket. "People here. People coming through."

"Can we stop this?" Eva asks.

"Stop what?"

"This. Can we go back? There's a real campground, a park service campground, just up the road. I saw a sign."

"Park service? They want, like, what? Ten bucks?"

"This is a little creepy."

"Come on. It's not that bad."

"That sheriff guy. Those guys in the bar. They know where we are."

"Those guys? They've never set a foot off pavement."

"You don't know that."

Mosquitoes hurl at them, invisible, screaming.

"I know everything," Ernie says.

"No, you don't. You don't know everything."

Ernie turns, pushing harder into the woods. Branches crack. "Yo, bear!" he yells. Eva follows the little black imprint he's made in the woods.

Ten minutes later Ernie thinks he hears something.

"Yo, bear?" Ernie calls out.

"Hey," a voice yells, "will you shut the hell up?"

"Sorry, man." Ernie trips over a tent rope.

"Asshole!" someone yells.

Eva stumbles into a clearing, the shoebox crushed and wet in her hands. In the moonlight, Ernie sits surrounded by tents and tarps and smoldering campfires.

"What is this?" Eva asks.

"This?" Ernie shrugs. "Now this, I think, is your market."

Fiona, back
at headquarters

Fish and Game district headquarters is a two-story office structure standing alone on the highway. It was originally a hunting supply store and still holds the smell of gunpowder. Fiona's desk sits among the desks of eight officers and four administrators. All share one huge picture window, looking across the highway into a huge pine swamp. Above the treetops, Fiona watches great billowing clouds drift east and south. She often wonders if they are the same clouds that, a week or two later, will be seen drifting above what was once her home. She starts thinking of the conversation she had with a friend she's made, a nurse, and how much she regretted it.

They'd had dinner, then a few pitchers, in a crowded local bar. The nurse friend complained for two hours about the drifters and shiftless drunks who the sheriff brought in, night after night, with the same sad stories—waffle-asses, she kept calling them, again and again. Fiona's nurse friend, drunk and slurring her speech, leaned over the table and said, "So, Fiona, why are you so angry?"

"Because I hate being stuck in an office," Fiona had blurted out. It all started spilling out of her, the crushing disappointment of being sent to an office assignment that rarely offered fieldwork. "Because I hate phony camaraderie. Because I deeply resent putting money into a can each time I get a cup of coffee. Because I loathe chipping in for birthday cards, and I can't stand signing them. And because I really, really hate the endless stream of sport fishermen and hunters coming in for permits. They ask the same stupid questions. They want to know where to go. They want to know if I've seen any elk. How should I know where the elk are? And why the hell would I tell them if I did? And because I hate filling out the permit forms. Each one feels like another one-pound brick tied around my neck. And I hate the chattiness and all the bureaucracy."

"Well, you're still new up here, so they're gonna dump the paperwork on you," the nurse said. "Same thing happened to me my first year up here."

"Yeah, I know."

"Still, you must really be unhappy."

"Let's forget it," Fiona said. What Fiona regrets now, staring out at the clouds from her desk, is not telling her nurse friend what makes her happy about her work—the rare chances to be out in the field, surveying wildlife, tracking down poachers and people who abuse the peninsula and its rightful owners. How she takes great pride in her field-work and finds the bureaucracy of office life to be utterly meaningless. She enjoys connecting the problem to the source, like the dead bear and Chief; and she was so excited to track down Chief and almost catch him. She was embarrassed and angry to have to report that he slipped away, and the consolation that he'd probably run back downland, like all the others, still left her particularly angry and upset.

Worsening her mood this morning, Fiona is assigned to type up the transcripts from a case she would have handled if she hadn't been sent after Chief. In a remote area outside of the Great Gulf Wilderness, her colleagues had recently tracked and arrested a bootleg surveyor—a woman with surveying equipment mapping out a stretch of unclaimed land. During the long seaplane ride back, the woman, named Gretchen Maloney, destroyed all the equipment, kicked out a panel on the plane, and broke one of the officer's noses. Under questioning, she suddenly changed course and lashed out at the people who contracted her—a ski resort development company setting its sights on a region that was being set aside for wildlife conservation. The case has huge ramifications for the peninsula's future, but for Fiona, there is no joy in typing it up.

Fiona is still staring out the window when a familiar beat-up pickup truck passes on the highway. Oh, yes, she thinks. I almost forgot about him. That doper campground ranger. What is his name? Sig? Dane? Probably headed up to Petrolia to score a nickel bag. Fiona looks down at the forms spread out across her desk—on a fishing permit application, the applicant has scribbled, "Where are the fish?" When she looks up again, she sees that the truck has pulled into the parking lot, almost lurching into the woods. The campground ranger—Dave, Donny, whatever—climbs out and walks with great purpose across the parking lot toward the office door.

As he enters the office, he smiles and waves. Surprising herself, she waves back.

"So I think I got something," he says, sitting on the edge of a steel chair. "I think I know where he is."

She looks at his name tag: Danny. Now she remembers. Park service.

"You think you know where who is?"

"Chief. The bear killer. I think I know where he is."

"You already said that."

"I did?"

"So, where is he?"

"There was a report this morning over the forest service radio from the Great Gulf Wilderness. There's eighty-six walk-in sites and a couple of lean-tos. I applied to work there, but somebody beat me to it. It's right on the ledges..."

"I know where Great Gulf Wilderness is," she says.

"Oh. Anyhow, the rangers there reported a number of stolen items at the Great Gulf campsite. Campers woke up and found a lot of their gear missing. Most of the stuff was ripped out of bags that were bear-hung. Looked like the bags were cut open."

"That could have been a bear, ranger. Bears get into bags all the time. People don't know how to hang bear bags anymore."

"But then later in the day, a mother and her kid described a large, heavy-set man who took off with their backpack. She was pretty pissed, said he left them up on the ridge, left them pretty lost. They made it down all right, but…"

"Did somebody go after him?"

"Who?"

"The man you're describing?"

"Um, no, not to my knowledge. The mom said when the clouds lifted, they could see for miles, and they couldn't see him anywhere. They thought he must've gone right over the edge."

Fiona closes the file on her desk, opens a drawer with one set of keys to remove another set of keys. "I know where he's going," she says, rising.

"Where's he going?" Danny says, following her to a gun rack locked in a glass case.

"He's going out to Grizzletown."

"Why would he go to Grizzletown?"

"All the dirt balls end up in Grizzletown. It's way in the bush and way off the map. They think they can get jobs there. They think there's a fleet of fishing boats and brand-new canneries waiting to hire them, and they get ten dollars an hour tax-free and fed three meals a day, and all these nice people can't wait for downlanders to come up and party with them. But there isn't, and they aren't, and they don't."

"Can I come with you?"

Fiona pulls down a shotgun. "Don't you have campers to check in back at your campground?"

"I'm sort of AWOL, I guess," Danny says, staring at the gun. Somehow, this time, it makes him feel safer. "I guess they'll just have to check themselves in."

FROM *THE ONLY PLANET GUIDE:* OUTER GRIZZLE AND THE EXTREMITIES

The volcano that erupted in 1972 sealed the only route beyond Black Harbor into the last stretch of wilds, referred to as Outer Grizzle. The few who have tried to cross the gulf, climb over the rubble of volcanic ruin, and enter this forbidding landscape have brought back wild tales of survival and loss. The weather that sweeps up from the ocean along the western mountain range is funneled straight across this last expanse of land. The surviving forest is made up of short, twisted scrub trees clinging to mounds of moss, which barely hold onto crumbling piles of rock pushed up from the ocean in one direction and the huge tectonic plates pushing up from the other. The farther one goes, the worse the weather and the terrain gets. The rocks pile in both directions down into the relentless sea. After seventy miles, this last strip of land narrows down into a thirty-mile strip of rock, called the extremities.

Somehow, this bleak wilderness is rumored to teem with life, including the region's largest bears; hundreds of huge seabirds; packs of roaming wolves, elk, moose, and beaver; and schools of fish that cloud the waters. Hunters and fishermen often attempt to sneak into this wilderness on foot, by boat, or by chartered plane. Permits are never issued for the territory beyond the gulf; despite this fact, it is estimated that more than three hundred people attempt entry each year. Of these, more than one hundred end up being rescued by air or by sea, and more than one hundred are "disappeared," never found by rescue personnel. Each year the forest service, fish and game, and other rescue operations lose between four and twenty rescuers. Needless to say, travel beyond the gulf is strongly discouraged and may be outlawed altogether in coming years.

Outer Grizzle Facts vs. Fiction: Somewhere out there is Grizzletown, the legendary settlement in a cove somewhere in the wilderness region. It does not appear on the few early military maps, has no consistent contact with the outside world, and is probably little more than a ghost town. As legend has it, it is a fully functioning town of several hundred lost souls with limited electricity, a working diner, and a bar built in a ruined cathedral (created by an earlier religious settlement). The settlement is believed to receive supplies from bootleggers traveling up the west coast by boat, exchanging food, liquor, and supplies for pelts and other raw materials extracted from the region. Other stories have it that it is completely self-sustaining, that communal workers harvest fish and vegetables from the bountiful surroundings, and that hippie leaders happily pay itinerant workers ten bucks an hour to support the labor force. Closer to the truth, military records indicate that they ran a small fishing operation there to supply the troops, and that it was later occupied by drifters who made it that far and never came back. Idealists, mystics, and survivalists all have their unique ideas of what Grizzletown represents, and some try to push on past Black Harbor to reach this utopian dream, with predictable results.

While Grizzletown is probably little more than a ghost town, other legends of the region abound. A favorite story among soldiers is the tale of a homesick private who "lost it" and escaped from his base, under a barbed wire fence, into the wilderness to the north. Three mornings later, a patrol reported finding the private's head, upper torso, and one arm attached to the top of the same barbed wire fence.

It is widely believed that this story, along with tales of mermaids and alien creatures, were manufactured by soldiers suffering through the tedium of army camp life in the wilds. The legend of the "Grizzarillo"—a huge, vicious bear with bulletproof armor that moves sixty miles an hour—is clearly an old soldier's tale.

New Age mystics also believe in a legend that a certain undefined "light energy" crosses the region at summer's end, and those who find themselves in its path gain powers of vision and healing. While this is clearly impossible, it is true that Outer Grizzle has no magnetic center whatsoever; airplane and nautical instruments go haywire the nearer they approach the land mass. Huge pools of aloe-like plants glow and change color, the result of unique saltwater algae mixing with glacial silt. A unique brand of quicksand called "quick-mud" along the coastlines changes form when the tide comes in on the western edges, sucking feet into the mud, the end of more than one unsuspecting beachcomber. It is true that shipwrecks and industrial waste of all sizes and shapes line the coast on both sides and that airplane and helicopter wreckage—military and nonmilitary—can be found throughout the region.

Disclaimer: *This guidebook suggests in the strongest possible terms that travelers who have made it to Black Harbor have completed their Grizzle Peninsula experience, and anyone who pushes beyond this point does so at great risk to their personal safety, no matter how experienced or well equipped they feel they are. The phrase used by locals for people who venture into the Outer Grizzle territory is "They've gone four-D"—the four Ds being disorientation, disappointment, disaster, and disappearance. It is far better to turn back from here than to plunge into this confusing, dangerous landscape, putting yourself at undue risk for an adventure with few rewards.*

Eva and Ernie in
the logging truck

Ernie and Eva are silent as the logging truck winds up the dirt road toward the Great Gulf. Ernie sits surrounded by a thick haze, the residue of the last binge before the music fair. Eva sits next to him, patching the side pocket of her backpack.

The truck goes around a bend, and the sun bursts through the clouds. "Look!" the driver, who picked them up on the spur road just a few miles outside the fairgrounds, yells. She's an older woman with long white hair and dreamcatcher earrings. She catches Ernie's eye in the rearview mirror and points ahead, across a sweep of metallic tundra and silver water draining everywhere.

The Great Gulf and its surrounding mountains are visible in the distance. Closer, a huge white mass, a volcano, fills half the sky. Ernie focuses on it, and all the dark thoughts drain from his mind.

"Sweet Jesus," he says.

"It's just a mountain," Eva says, pulling needle through nylon.

"I hope the sky opens up when we're in there," Ernie says. "I hope we see it up close."

Eva shrugs, not looking up. The clouds quickly seal themselves around the summit, still many miles away. The hangover pours itself back into Ernie, but he knows it will evaporate in time. Three or four days out on the trail, and it will be gone. The driver pulls over on a bridge. She pulls a lever, and the truck door exhales.

"Here you go," she says. "The trail to Grizzletown."

"Where?" Eva asks.

"You're headed right up there someplace." She points to a raging torrent of green water ripping a gap between two steep ledges. "That's Grizzle Pass. That's where the road used to go before the volcano blew. Now you go by trail."

"But there's no trail," Eva says.

The driver looks at Eva like she's crazy.

"There are no trails anywhere, sweetie," the driver says. "This is the wilderness."

"Thanks for the lift," Ernie says, climbing down.

"The Great Gulf Wilderness is a real nice park, you know. They got campsites and trails and stuff. It's a whole lot better for hiking."

"Thanks," Eva says.

"Yeah, but don't go trying to sneak in there. Forest service catches you in the Great Gulf Wilderness without a permit, you're out two hundred bucks."

"Okay," Ernie says.

"Try to stay up high," the driver continues. "Look for the goat paths. When you hit the valley, you'll see the remains of the road. Good luck to ya. You know how to hang your food?"

"Yep," Ernie says, taking Eva's pack.

"And make a lot of noise," the driver says. "There's a lot of traffic up there this time of year."

"Traffic?" Eva asks. The truck's door closes.

Eva follows Ernie along a sandbar at a creek's edge. In fifty yards the sandbar gives way to water. They climb onto a parallel ledge that follows the rushing water another twenty yards, then crumbles into the water. Ernie pushes into a wall of stubbled green plants. They're a foot over his head and push him back. He pushes harder, and they give way. Soon he's pulling himself up a steep, slick incline through tangled shoots. Eva follows without asking any questions. In thirty minutes they break into something like a sloping meadow, where the brush is only waist deep. Every so often they break into a depression in the plants where something large and heavy was rolling around fairly recently. They can see the park road far below them, and they can hear the gurgling cascade of the creek. Sparkling silver clouds rotate just feet above their heads, brushing against the rocky red peaks all around them.

"Do you have any idea where we're going?" Eva asks.

"Just west, and north," Ernie says. "We break over this ridge, then the next one, along the base of the volcano. We follow the creek and stay above the rock piles, where the road used to go. After that there's a valley. It's supposed to be unbelievably beautiful. We follow the valley down to Grizzletown."

"This doesn't seem very passable," Eva says. "There's no trail."

"I think we just follow the creek," Ernie says. "If we stay up here, we should be all right." Ernie looks around. There's a glacier somewhere just over the next ridge, emitting an eerie phosphorous light.

"I read someplace that the mountains out here are so big that they generate their own weather. The climate change is so severe from the ocean, up the steep slopes, and around all these deep glaciers and ice that it all creates these huge columns of vapor. So it's like this huge block of energy, all jutting out into the ocean."

"Wow," Eva says. She's squinting up at the sky, which is increasingly menacing.

"Yeah, and these storms come up through the gulf, these huge storms, and they wrap around the mountains. And before you know it, they're just spinning around it in circles, just spinning. For days and days. Like this rain here? This rainstorm?" Ernie holds out his hands as big, cold, driven drops splash against them. "This rainstorm was probably here last night. And will probably be here again tomorrow morning."

"That's great," Eva says. She's pulling on her poncho.

"That's unless, of course, one of these serious numbers come along. I think the soldiers back in the war called it the 'Upland Express.' A really huge thing, really high up, a high-pressure thing. They come in from way down at the end of the peninsula or someplace, and they push down onto these storms. And then it's like, you know, all bets are off. Summer blizzards. Serious wind disturbances. Windstorms. Really powerful stuff."

The rain starts driving down harder.

"I don't know. I know it sounds really stupid."

"I think it is really powerful, what you just said," Eva says.

"Really?" Ernie says.

"Really. It's energy. It's all this energy up here."

Ernie pulls his own anorak around him; he's already soaked. "Well, I guess we should get moving again," he says.

They push up the ledges for hours. They spot a clear ledge jutting out over a cliff and climb down to it. It's a fully exposed shoulder of polished rock, ten feet wide and twenty feet long, dropping steeply on either side to the rushing creek several hundred feet below. From the ledge they can clearly see that there is no beautiful valley anywhere in their near future, that there is another range to cross. The sides of the gorge are steep and filled with deep brush. But for the moment, the rain has stopped, and early evening sunlight creeps into the gorge. A beautiful, clear creek bubbles icy fresh water just a few yards downhill. They set up the tent, tying the lines off on large, flat rocks, and hang their soaked raingear to dry.

They boil noodles on the camp stove. Looking at the stark ridges above them, Eva says, "Do you really think this is a safe spot?"

"I think a bear would have a hell of a time climbing up here, if that's what you mean," Ernie says.

"It's not just the bears," Eva says. She scans her surroundings in silence. "I don't know. It just gives me chills. It's like, I can feel that volcano. We've pushed so far, we're so far out there now. We're really cut off here."

"Grizzletown will be great, you'll see," Ernie says. "It's going to be a great big natural community living off the land. They don't need anything from the rest of the world. It just sounds so great," Ernie says. "I really think we're going to find our kind of people out there."

"I don't know," she says.

After dinner, Ernie climbs up through the brush to hang their food bag a safe distance from the tent. He comes across the bleached skull of a ram, its horns perfectly intact, lying face down in the grass.

"Eva," he says, "you gotta check this out."

She walks up, looks, and turns away. "Why did you need to show me that?" she says.

"I don't know. I've just never seen anything like it."

Eva walks back to the tent. In the still evening air, Ernie stares down into the skull for a long time. The eye sockets, though inverted, stare back. Suddenly he is consumed with thirst. He takes the bag a little farther up the hill, then climbs down to stick his head in the icy creek for as long as he can hold it there. The wind is starting to pick up again. The last light fades from the gorge. Eva is sitting on a large rock by the stove, boiling water for tea. He sits down on the rock across from her.

"I'm sorry about the skull. I sort of thought it was interesting."

"Ernie, can I ask you something?"

"Sure."

 "Why are you drinking again?"

"Because I'm thirsty."

"I don't mean the water."

"Me either."

"I'm serious."

"Me too."

"Can you try to stop? For good?"

"Unless there's a bar under this rock, I'm stopped at the moment."

"No, like, when we get to Grizzletown? And when we go back home?"

Ernie tries to think of how many hours it's been and realizes he can't; he figured he'd be out in the backcountry for three or four days and would see how it goes. He went without a drink for one night on the road with Rosemarie and Corinne and held out for a few nights here and there.

"I can absolutely try."

"It's just that you're a totally different person when you're not drinking. It's like you're here. Totally. Whatever 'here' is."

"Okay."

"When you called me from the road, you told me you were sober, like, three times. Were you really sober?"

"I was trying to be," Ernie says. "I guess maybe I wasn't."

"Can you try now?"

"I'll try."

"Thank you."

"Sure," Ernie says. "I'll give it a go."

The wind continues to pick up. Ernie's rain cover flips off the line and flies straight up the gorge like a torn parachute. They gather the rest of the raingear and climb into the tent. The wind keeps blowing. By midnight the tent is shuddering, the fly is flapping so loudly it's screaming, and the tent poles are bending down all around them.

"Do you think we're going to get blown off the ledge?" Eva yells, lying next to him in her sleeping bag.

"I think it's definitely possible," Ernie yells back.

"Is there anything we can do?"

"I don't think so. Just wait it out, I guess."

Something rattles away down the ledge; probably one of the rocks Ernie used to tie down the tent. The flapping grows louder. The tent bends down further around them.

"I think you're finally starting to wear me down," Eva yells.

"What?"

"You can put your arm around me now," she yells.

Somewhere in the night, the roaring air stills itself; Ernie can hear it hurtling up the slopes of the mountains, then fading away into the next valley. He falls into a deep sleep but keeps his arm around Eva.

Ernie wakes up to sunlight gleaming through the tent. He's alone; Eva's crumpled sleeping bag lies open beside him. He's sure he dreamed the windstorm, then realizes that the sunlight means the tent fly is gone. Ernie rolls over and peers out through the tent flap. He sees Eva from the back, at a distance. She's squatting down by the creek, scooping up icy water and rubbing it into her arms and neck. Condensation rises from her breath and the cold water on her skin. Inside his warm sleeping bag, he shudders; he could never do that.

Ernie pretends to wake up when she climbs back up to the tent, her hair dripping wet. As he struggles to disengage himself from his sleeping bag and climb out of the tent, he's reminded again of age; his whole body seems to fail him. His once-boundless hamstrings don't seem to work. He hobbles to the rock next to where Eva has set up the cook stove.

"Man," he says, trying to sit down.

"You need to breathe," she says, stirring oatmeal into the boiling water. "You need to breathe. You'll feel better."

"Yeah," Ernie says.

"The tent fly is gone. Completely. Just ripped off and went."

"Huh."

Eva squints up the ledges to the north. Close by, sunlight streams in through a few gaps. Farther down, a new row of storm clouds creeps down the ledges. They hover over shimmering wet walls of steep rock, glowing with water from the previous day's soaking. Eva takes a deep breath.

"So, I've been trying to find my light this morning."

"Your light?" Ernie asks, looking around the campsite.

"Yeah, you know, my energy? My direction? Whatever. Anyhow, I'm having a difficult time finding it here." She shrugs in the direction of the wilderness ahead. "I just don't know if it's up there."

"Yeah," Ernie says, looking at the jagged rocks between them and the surging gully at the canyon floor. "It looks pretty impenetrable."

"I didn't mean like that."

"Oh."

"But it's like, when my energy, when my light is in a certain place, I can follow it. Do you know what I'm saying?" She looks distressed, Ernie thinks. Genuinely upset.

"I think maybe I know what you're saying."

Ernie has no idea what she's saying. He looks up the valley. They were so close. Another couple of days, and they would be in Grizzletown—the great north valley, the wolves howling at midnight, the spinning colors, and the other side of this great mountain. He would have been working by day's end, ten bucks an hour, no taxes. They would have met cool people in Grizzletown and lived in an abandoned old house and shared things. They'd pack up and hike out just before the snow hits and return home with a thousand bucks and a world of stories, ready to start a new life together. Ernie shrugs. He rubs the back of his legs, trying to get the feeling back.

"You need to breathe," Eva says, forcing a smile.

They pack up the tent and turn to the faint hint of a goat trail. Eva steps out first and continues deeper into the wilderness, toward Grizzletown.

"I thought you wanted to head back?" Ernie says.

"I do, eventually. But not until we get to check out Grizzletown."

Ernie follows her. Ten steps from their campsite, Ernie looks down and shudders. In the mud prints left by their boots the day before are larger, wider imprints, like somebody dug out their footprints and filled them with water. The prints follow theirs, then turn up the hill just above where they camped. Eva sees them too.

"How long ago?" she asks.

"Maybe early this morning," Ernie says. "Maybe last night." They turn, moving more briskly through the brush, down the hill. "Yo, bear!" Ernie says firmly.

"Yo! Bear!" Eva starts calling out. They follow the big bear's tracks. The big mountains are now clear and visible, locked in their own haze. Warm sunlight seeps through in little spotlights, spraying the valley floor in shimmering green light.

"What will we do when we get to Grizzletown?" Ernie asks.

"I think I'll be ready for a shower," Eva says. "A shower and a warm bed. And a nice dinner. I wonder if they have a restaurant." Eva leans her head against his shoulder as they walk, and he puts his arm around her shoulder again.

"The weather's turning again," Ernie says.

It's early evening. Ernie is following Eva down to the faint trace that used to be the road, but which is now reduced to a mud strip with patches of weeds and pools of gravel, stretching like a faint ribbon down the center of a large, sloping valley. Heavy rains are swirling down from the peaks behind them. The sky seems darker and colder. Eva puts her pack down and shakes her head.

"I don't know. All of a sudden I've just got a seriously bad energy thing going on here."

"We're so close," Ernie says. "But do you want to turn back? We can still turn back. If you want to."

It starts raining in sheets. Eva hangs her head and shuffles forward. Ernie tries pointing out how beautiful the bowl of mountains surrounding them is, the steep ravines covered in shiny metallic black rock and green tundra. They find a protective cove of tangled bushes. They are still at a high elevation, far above the tree line, close under the serrated ridge of peaks they will pass the next day on the last leg of the trip to Grizzletown. They unroll their soggy tent and sleeping bags and cook dinner.

The rain stops, but dense new clouds billow over the summits. Ernie looks down at his tin plate and sees little gray flecks of powder gathering on his noodles. The sky lights up suddenly with angry red ripples against the deep gray clouds. A deep rumble like distant thunder echoes ominously off the high cliffs, and the ground around them starts to make large cracking noises.

"It's just the volcano," Ernie tries to say, matter-of-factly, over the rumble. He looks up at what he realizes is a huge, billowing, black cloud of ash coming down the valley, reaching for them. "I think we should get in the tent."

Without the fly, huge black clumps settle on the tent's surface, and it quickly goes black. There's a choking smell of sulfur. Eva buries her head next to him, and he holds on to her, as tightly as he can, until it all goes black.

Chief at the cathedral

As the blow of plume and ash engulfs the rest of the peninsula, a thick stream of cold, foggy vapor crawls slowly down the volcano walls, through the dense forest, and down the valley toward the settlement of Grizzletown. It reaches hot gray fingers across the marsh flats, mixes with salt-thick swamp gasses, and darkens the blackness of the night. In the smoky encampments surrounding the settlement, it picks up the smoke of damp campfires and the smell of dead fish. Arriving just as the sun sets, the vapors wind slowly through Grizzletown's few streets, then twist themselves around and into the Cathedral Saloon. Inside, puddles of keg beer and the stale smoke of thousands of cigarettes wash out the smell of the sulfur. In the interior, a long plank bar runs across the center of the dim-lit, steam-choked room. Boards on sawhorses hand-cut from old pews serve as tables, and crates serve as chairs, spread haphazardly around the bar. The surface of each table has been carved repeatedly with coded names and initials and slogans. Two old men in tattered army fatigues stare at Chief suspiciously, then stare down into their beers. Human forms slump around several of the tables, mumbling plans to one another, shrouded in vapor that nobody seems aware of.

A tall man enters the Cathedral Saloon, dressed in a long bearskin coat. Owl-feather earrings, a waxed beard, and braided hair hang from his face. Even in the darkness of the bar, he quickly selects and crosses to his target: two overweight men in worn-out parkas, one of whom waves him over to the farthest table. He strides across the floor in his boots, heel to toe, with great deliberation, although no one else in the bar takes any notice of him.

"Scout! Over here!" yells one of the men. He slides the pitcher and a glass down the table.

Scout takes the pitcher and glass, straddles the bench, and nods to his acquaintance. "Wolf." He pours beer into the glass, drinks it, wipes the foam from his mouth, and pours himself another. Then he turns to Wolf and the stranger sitting across the table. "Worked up quite a little thirst today. Taking care of a little nasty business."

"Scout here's a trapper," Wolf says to his friend. "Wolf, this here's Chief. I knew Chief out at the camp outside Portia."

"How you doing," Chief says. Chief's been drinking since he stumbled out of the wilderness. Still wild-eyed with terror, he came across an encampment of little shacks made of plywood and blue tarps on the beach. Everybody there knew Wolf, and everybody knew where he'd be: "In the Cathedral Saloon," they said. "Just keep moving down the beach. It's like an old cathedral with a 'bar' sign over the door. You can't miss it. He'll be there."

"I'm doing just fine," Scout says now. "Took care of a little problem I had up Dead Soldier Creek with a moocher." He drains the beer dramatically and reaches for the pitcher again, but the pitcher is empty. He stares into the foam collected on the bottom of the pitcher. "You don't want to go mooching on old Scout, that's for sure." He puts the empty pitcher on the table and pushes it across the scarred table to Chief. "You'll make old Scout mighty thirsty."

"Chief was sort of a head man at the camp back in Portia," Wolf says as Chief goes to buy a pitcher. Chief found a wallet with eighty dollars in the bag he took, but it's already down to fifteen. "He sort of kept an eye on things."

"Well, he ain't gonna be head man in Grizzletown, that's for sure," Scout said. "We live by a different code of law here."

"I know," Wolf says. "It looks like he got into a little trouble up in Portia. A confrontation with the authorities."

"Is that right," Scout says as Chief returns with the pitcher and offers it to Scout first. "I understand you've had a little trouble with the law."

Chief can't help but smile at this. "Apparently Fish and Game didn't appreciate the way I was running things," Chief says. "Some little waffle-ass weasel ratted me out." Chief drinks a chug of beer down, the foam sticking to his beard. "They didn't count on the challenges of tracking a man of my skill set."

"Well, your talents, as you put it, may serve you well here. We'll just have to see. Fish and Game don't come out here much. They know what we stand for. Out here we don't need their rule of law. If something needs to be done, we take it into our own hands. Understood?"

"Chief thought maybe he could get himself work out here, maybe some fish factory work."

Scout looks at them skeptically. "Now you know there ain't no work out here for downlanders. All the canneries shut down when the road got buried. The fleet sailed on."

"Yeah," Wolf says. "I pretty much told him there weren't much use in trying."

"You want to survive out here, you're going to have to learn some things." Before Chief can reach for the pitcher, Scout drains it again. "Back in wherever, you may have been Chief, but here in Grizzletown, you're just a little fella now. You dig?"

"Sure thing," Chief says. The conversation starts to burn him. The terror from his days stumbling and bushwhacking through the wilderness has drained him, and he starts filling up with rage again. He picks up the pitcher and walks to the bar. I'm just gonna have to establish myself again, Chief thinks to himself, pressing his fingers against the revolver stuffed in his pants. My luck's going to have to change. I'm just going to have to find a way to change it.

Ernie and Eva under the volcano

Ernie and Eva crawl out of their tent to find everything covered in an inch of thick gray silt. By the time they break camp, they are coated in it. The rains begin to fall again by midmorning. As they travel down through the valley, the rainwater smears the blanket of powder down the surrounding cliffs. Beneath the ash, the newly exposed tundra has changed, overnight, from its summer green to deep crimson red.

Shuffling slowly next to him, her face wrapped in an ash-caked bandanna, Eva finally speaks. "Are we going to die up here?"

"I think if the volcano was really going to blow, we would be pretty dead or something," Ernie says. That didn't sound very convincing, he thinks to himself. "I'm pretty sure that was like, a little eruption or something."

Eva looks back toward the mountain pass they crossed through the day before; a dense fog or smoke appears to be streaming out of it and settling on the valley floor behind them.

"Are we going to be able to get out?"

"We'll figure out a way. There's plenty of cool people in Grizzletown, I'm sure of it. They'll know how to pack out of here."

Eva shrugs and looks away, hugging her arms to her chest. Ernie walks at a distance from her, watching the light on the cliffs above.

As the road bends down around a corner, they look out onto the town. Ernie is surprised—it's not at all what he was led to believe. There are a few miserable-looking sheet metal factories that have clearly been closed for a long time and some ramshackle, run-down apartment buildings, like housing projects, spread out in a circle around what looks like a crumbling, large church. A strand of tarp shacks stretches out on a sandy bluff, facing the sea. From here they can see shrouded forms huddled around smoky fires. A long row of docks with rusting steel cranes juts out into a harbor. The shells of three or four trawlers lie rusting in dry dock next to roofless buildings; beyond this, in the oily, shimmering harbor, there are no boats anywhere to be seen.

"So this is Grizzletown, I guess," Ernie says.

On the town's perimeter, where the crumbling reminders of the road turn down what might be a main street, they pass an old diner. Behind it, on the other side of a long clearing, there is a cabin with a painted orange "for rent" sign nailed to the door. Ernie enters the diner. The owner, an old man in suspenders and a huge beard, tells Ernie that the diner's closed until breakfast but the cabin's available, if they want it, for the night.

"There's some weather coming in," the old man says. "It's awful cozy, hot shower and firewood for the stove, and it's ten dollars a night. Just make sure you look both ways when you get up. That's an emergency airstrip we run over there next to it. You don't want to get run over by no airplane."

"How often do planes make emergency landings here?" Ernie asks.

"What, here? Never."

Ernie looks out the diner window and sees Eva sitting on her backpack, her eyes closed. He pays for the cabin, takes the keys, and turns to the door.

"Kitchen opens at six," the owner says. "Make sure you come in the morning for a pancake."

The cabin has a huge four-poster bed covered in quilts, a large stone fireplace stacked with a cord of wood, and a table with two chairs. Ernie builds a big fire while Eva takes a shower.

"You know," he says to Eva, "I might just have two pancakes."

"The fire feels good," Eva says. She's wrapped herself in the quilt. She's pulled on ragg wool mittens and a hat she's brought with her, thousands of miles, in the bottom of her backpack, for this moment.

"This is nice," Ernie says. "We needed to take a rest."

"We're going to get stuck here," Eva says. "We're never going to be able to hike out of here. If that volcano keeps going, the pass is gone, and we'll be stuck in this...place."

"We'll be okay."

"We're never going to make it out of here," she says, pulling the quilt still tighter around herself. Her eyes close, and her head nods forward; she slowly leans back and falls into a deep sleep. Ernie sits up for some time, listening for the volcano to blow again, imagining the ash slowly encircling them. When he wakes up, in the bed beside Eva, the cabin's windows are sealed in ash.

In the early morning, two old men in old army fatigues with drooping white beards sit at the diner counter drinking mugs of coffee. Eva and Ernie sit down at a booth by the picture window. From their seats, above long-dormant gas pumps, they can see low-hanging white clouds billowing quickly across the sky, dragging little strips of vapor through the tops of the pine trees. The owner appears in a crumpled apron behind the counter.

"Sleep good?" he asks.

"Very well, thank you," Ernie responds.

"I got the pancake and coffee. That's all I got."

"I'll have the pancakes."

"Right. The pancake."

"Is there more than one pancake?"

"You don't want more than one pancake."

"Actually, I'm pretty hungry."

"I'll bring you the pancake. You want a second pancake, I'll bring you another. You, miss?"

"Do you have any oatmeal? And some black tea?"

"Nope. All we got right now is the pancake and some coffee beans. Been that way some time now. We're waiting for a boat to come in soon. We're running out of everything." He disappears behind the counter.

The two men at the counter, who have been watching the exchange, turn to look at Ernie.

"You folks hiking back out today?" one asks.

"Not just yet," Ernie says. "Actually, we just got here."

"What, you looking for work?"

"Yeah, actually," Ernie says. "Do you know anybody who's hiring?"

The two men look at each other and shrug.

"Thing is," one says, "people come up here looking for work all the time. There ain't no work out here. Ain't been nothing for years. Even for the locals."

"Oh," Ernie says.

"If you're thinking of turning right around though, I'd wait a spell" the second one says. "Don't look so good, the pass right now. Don't know if the volcano's going to keep blowing or not. The pass is all socked in."

"We aren't in such a big hurry."

The two men stare down into their mugs. Then the second one says, "You wait a bit, you'll be okay."

The owner returns from behind the counter with two mugs of coffee and a huge pancake six inches high, flopping off the sides of a large china plate.

"Here's the pancake," he says, putting it down in front of Ernie with two hands. "You want another one, you just give a holler."

Eva holds the coffee mug and stares out the window at the sky. "You're not going to eat that whole thing, are you?" she asks.

Ernie digs in. Hot, fluffy. At this moment, it is the best thing he's ever tasted.

"So," Ernie says, "maybe we can figure out another way out of here."

The two men stare out the window, just above Eva and Ernie. They all watch the clouds of ash grow darker and creep lower, pressing down against the thick forest and inching in gray vertical strips across the empty roadway.

"Hey," Ernie says, "do you guys know an alternate trail out of here? Other than the pass?"

"You mean for walking out?"

"Yeah, you know. A forest service road or a trail."

"I wouldn't go walking out today," one says. "Not with the volcano still blowing and all."

"There's a forest service road runs right up behind the old airstrip, up and over the ridge," the other one says. "I wouldn't go trying to walk out that way though."

"You'll want to watch out for bears around here," the first man says. "You'll be better off sticking to the old road."

"Oh, god," Eva says.

Ernie looks up from the huge pancake, half-finished, to see what she's looking at. Flakes of ash—huge white ones— whip around the gas pumps and stick to the pavement.

"Course, looking now like nobody's going nowhere for a spell," one of the men says.

The ash plasters itself to the cabin's damp windowpane; the world outside swirls from gray to white. Cold, and dizzy from his enormous breakfast, Ernie throws a log on the fire. Eva sits on the bed, a blanket wrapped around her shoulders, shivering.

"It'll blow out," Ernie says. "They say it does this all the time."

"It's bigger than that."

"Bigger?"

"It's caught us. We're stuck here."

"I don't think anything's caught us, not yet."

"I think maybe you wanted to get caught."

"I'm not really sure what 'caught' is," Ernie says, trying not to sound doubtful.

"I think you wanted to come out here, just to get away from everything else. I don't think it was going to be this great and beautiful and magical place, like you said. There's no jobs here, no magical communal houses, and all these beautiful people living off the land. There's no light here. I think you knew this all along. I think you wanted me to come out here because you want to disappear from the world, and you wanted to take me with you."

Ernie looks out the window at the ash piling onto the pine boughs across the airstrip like snow.

"I just like it so much here. I just want to keep going to the end. It's magical."

"It's not magical."

"It's not?"

Eva shrugs. "You just wanted to disappear. Just like everybody here. The disappeared."

"Maybe you're right," Ernie says, closing his eyes, imagining the ash piling on top of them like a blanket.

*

Hours later, Ernie sits up. Eva is on the edge of the bed, hands clasped in her lap.

"Wow, that was weird," Ernie says. "I must have fallen asleep."

"You were talking," Eva says.

"Did I say something funny?"

"No."

Ernie looks at the film of light coming through the cabin windows. "Look, the sun's out. Let's just go for a walk, huh? It's stopped now, it's going to clear. Let's go for one more little hike. There's maybe an inch of ash out there, right? We'll find the forest road those guys told us about. It'll be beautiful. I'll bet by the time we come back, the ash will blow off. And we'll gather our things, and we'll just pack right out of here. We'll just push on through the pass. In three days we'll be back in Petrolia. You can fly home from there if you want to, or maybe we can get your car fixed and you can drive home. You can do what you want to."

Eva pushes her hair back from her face but says nothing.

"What do you say. Little hike?"

"You go," Eva says. "I really need to think."

The ash has stopped falling from the sky. Ernie crunches toward the forest road the men mentioned, then, remembering their warning, he changes his mind midway across the airstrip. The temperature has plummeted. He's wrapped in every layer he could find on the way to the door—three shirts, a fleece pullover, the damp hooded anorak, socks over his hands, and a T-shirt over his head. Walking briskly, he circles back around the diner and sets off toward the road, following it back to the steel bridge they crossed the day before. The bridge is a half-mile down the road; by the time he reaches it, he feels completely alone. The view is startling— a winding creek framed by sandbars draped in fresh volcanic powder, framed by six-foot bluffs and neat rows of birch and pine trees, all winding up a lonely hill to some blue-gray mountains, many miles up, caked in frosting. Without thinking, Ernie climbs down the embankment, then the bluff, and starts north on the sandbank. The sand is hard by the crinkling water, running over billions of blue and brown rocks from the mountains ahead, Ernie guesses, then rolling them all the way to the sea behind him.

Eva's right, really, Ernie thinks. I'm useless. If the volcano really has stopped, if we're not socked in up here forever, I'll help her get back home. I'll keep my mouth shut. I'll give her my last hundred bucks for an airplane ticket, and then I'll be on my way. Maybe I'll come back here, even.

Suddenly a huge blue hole rips open in the sky, pouring radiant sunshine onto Ernie and sparkling the water and trees. Little drifts of ash blow in curled waves up the creek around him, filling in his footprints. He's walked two miles, possibly three, and around several bends in the river. He turns around; the bridge is invisible, and his tracks are fading fast. The sunshine has blinded him for a moment.

In the woods something bright red and brown sparkles in the ash; he moves toward it. He stops twenty feet away from a moose, evidently a baby, that has very recently been disemboweled. It lies on its back, its legs splayed open and twisted. Steam rises from a gaping wound in its abdomen; blood, flesh, and clumps of hair are splattered on the ash and the birch bark. The moose's head is twisted sideways; one black eye stares up at Ernie, "Why?" Squinting, Ernie scans the surrounding woods, but sees no tracks, no signs of a new attack. He backs out slowly, never turning his back on the scene, and stumbles a hundred yards back downstream; then he takes off running for the bridge.

In front of the diner, he sees one of the men from the diner talking to a huge man in an orange snowsuit, a gun resting on his shoulder. The diner men are drinking cans of beer. The ash slides off the roof, falling in a thump to the ground.

"They think that's it, the 'ruption's over," one of the men says. "And they say the weather's blowing over. At least for a couple days."

"Thanks," Ernie says, turning.

"You want a beer?"

"Uh, no," Ernie says. "No, thanks."

He runs for the cabin and swings the door open. She's not there; she probably went into town, he reasons. Maybe she went to try to find a pay phone, to call David, to get some guidance. There's no pay phones here, but it certainly doesn't matter. There's nothing he can do to stop her. Ernie sits on the porch, waiting for Eva. A beer would certainly be nice right now, he thinks. It might help him relax. Just a beer or two. He doesn't need to get drunk. Ernie looks down the street and sees the neon "bar" sign glowing above the door of the Cathedral Saloon. Yeah, this place is a real crap hole, I guess, he thinks to himself. Just another line of crap I followed, and look where it got me. But that bar there, now that looks interesting. I can certainly go check it out, Ernie thinks. There's no harm in just taking a look inside, seeing what's inside that big smoky bar.

Fiona and Danny arrive
by seaplane

"So what gave you the stupid idea to come up here by yourself and become a fish and game warden?" Danny asks.

Danny is in a cheerful mood, in part because he's survived a flight in a seaplane that circled a volcano that blew the day before, then blew a second time while they were in the air. The turbulence and the plane's sputtering terrified him; now free, and following Fiona on the climb up from the cove where they were deposited, he feels light-headed. The old dirt road they've discovered will take them into Grizzletown from the north. After trekking to the top of the embankment and pushing through the brush to find the trail, they're covered in gray volcanic ash. Despite the conditions and the job ahead of them, Danny finds himself uncontrollably chatty, and he peppers Fiona with questions for a half-hour.

"It doesn't matter why I came," Fiona says, pulling a clump of the gray matter from her hair. She turns to walk up the dirt road. "I just came."

"Oh yeah? Did you come up with a friend or something? I mean, I'm just curious. We got a long walk ahead of us."

"It doesn't matter who I came up with."

"Oh yeah? Did something happen?"

"Something happened when a helicopter disappeared while trying to rescue some stupid-ass lost downlander nouveau-survivalist assholes who got themselves stuck out on the rocks out past here."

"Oh. I'm really sorry."

"Don't be. It happens all the time. They lose three or four choppers out here every summer trying to save the lives of hundreds of these idiots who have no business being out here, who have no respect for this place."

As a new band of rain sweeps in off the ocean, Danny pulls his poncho from his backpack and offers it to Fiona.

"Well, I'm sorry about your friend."

"It wasn't my friend. It was my brother," Fiona says. "And I've got my own raingear, thank you."

They cross over a ledge, climbing over a spray of bleached logs, then enter a cove. The rain stops. Smoke rises from a dense block of fir trees, rising and twisting into a low bank of clouds. Everything—the beach, the rocks, the trees—is coated in a thin film of ash.

"I'm real sorry about your brother," Danny says, trailing Fiona by a few steps. "You must have been close."

"I hadn't seen him in years," she says without turning.

"Oh."

Fiona stops for a moment, staring out into the cove, into the sea. It is impossible for Danny to determine where the sky ends and the sea begins and the swirling clouds stop and the puffs of smoke and ash start.

"But we *were* close, you know? We were really close. When we were little, everybody thought we were twin boys, even though we were two years apart. We were the same size, we wore the same hand-me-down clothes. We were shaggy, which kept other kids away from us. But we liked it that way. We only relied on each other. When our dad died, when our mom died, when our uncle shot our dog, when the house got sold, when we got passed around, we relied on each other. It was safer that way. We kept each other safe."

She starts walking along the waterline, following a strand of tangled kelp and rocks—the high-water markings weaving an S across the sand—and he follows her steps.

"They knew we were inseparable. But they had to separate us. My brother got sent off to a military academy, and I got sent to a boarding school. But we wrote letters, and we figured out how to call each other every once in a while. I don't think he ever realized how much those calls meant to me. He was always so upbeat. At fourteen, at fifteen, he was always figuring out something, how one day he'd get a house somewhere, or I'd get a house somewhere, and we'd hang out in the back yard and have a bunch of dogs.

"But what happened was—I eventually lost touch with him. I fell in with these kids at the boarding school who were really skilled at making all the pain go away. For them, life was a party. And the party was really impossible to resist, you know? So I became one of them, or I pretended I was one of them. And for a while, I was good at it. And things went from party to party, and then to something far worse. For them, when things got real bad, they could always go home. But where could I go? So they all went home. And I ended up strung out on a park bench."

Danny struggles for something to say. He tries to picture another Fiona, strung out, huddled on a park bench, but he can't. He is pushing, huffing, just to keep up with her, even though she is carrying the rifle and gear, scanning the tree line ahead.

"Wow," Danny says. "That sounds pretty bad."

"Actually, that wasn't the bad part. The park bench wasn't that bad. It was sheltered by bushes that kept the wind out, and I learned how to make myself invisible. There were four guys who sat around the chess tables nearby all day and night with needles in their arms or their ankles, and it sounds crazy, but they kept an eye on me, and they were sharing people. I know that sounds bad, but it was actually really good, they were good people, they were sharing people. I learned how to be silent, invisible. I learned how to take inventory. I could walk into a crowded bar, assess the dangers, the variables, slip into the bathroom, wash up, grab a couple bottles of beer from a distracted drunk, and slip out without anyone knowing. Living out there, a lot of the time, I was cold and hungry, but you know what? Everybody's cold and hungry.

"You know what really kept me going? There was a pay phone next to the park, near the bench where I was sleeping, and every once in a while, that phone would start ringing. It would ring and ring. And every so often, I imagined it was my brother calling me, to cheer me up, to lift my spirits. Or maybe he was calling to tell me he was coming to get me. Sometimes I imagined standing there at that pay phone, laughing into the receiver, listening to my brother and his big plans. I lay there, huddled and shivering on that bench, not wanting to get up and walk over and pick up that receiver because I wanted it to be him so bad, but I knew it was probably just a wrong number. That kept me going for a while there. But then the phone stopped ringing."

"So, can I ask" Danny said, "I mean, how did you get out of that situation?"

"There was this very nice, very straight-up-looking guy who came and hung out with the chess-table guys; it turned out he was a dealer. He came over and said hello every now and then, nothing more. Then one time he came over and asked me if I wanted a job delivering things. 'What about them?' I said, pointing back to the guys at the table. 'They're too far gone,' he said. 'The cops would pick them up in a second.' For some reason I liked this guy, he had a charming normalcy about him. I delivered for him for a while, and then one day I just ended up living with him."

"Wow," Danny says. "That must have been a relief. I mean, after living in the park."

"In some ways, yes. In some ways, it was a lot worse," Fiona says. "Anyhow, somehow, my brother tracked me down. It turned out he was up here in the military, and then he stayed up here to work rescue. We wrote and talked on the phone. We made a plan for me to get out of that life, to come up here. He was going to get a house. We were going to get a dog.

"And that," Fiona says, shifting the rifle from her left shoulder her right hand, "is how, I guess, my brother helped me get out of that world down there and get up to this world up here."

Fiona turns to Danny and stares at him for a moment, which feels like the first time they've made eye contact, and it startles him.

"Hey, thanks for listening," she says. "Since my brother, I never really get to talk to anybody about anything."

"Oh! Yeah," he says, not sure what to say in response. "Hey, how long did you say you've been up here?"

"I didn't."

"Oh yeah. That's cool. You just seem like you've been up here a long time."

"I came here in April. For training."

"No way. April of this year?"

"Yep. Just a few months ago."

"No offense, but you seem like you've been up here a long time."

"I feel like I've been here a long time."

Fiona turns back toward the forest line they are approaching, the backs of a few boarded-up outbuildings, an old, rusted pickup with no tires.

"Anyhow, enough chit-chat for now," Fiona says. "We have a job to do."

Danny looks at the settlement unfolding just beyond the trees. There's something large and round and manmade just beyond the little circle of buildings.

"What is that?" he asks.

"That's the cathedral. That's where he's going to be."

"How do you know?"

"Because that, according to reports, is where they all end up."

She reaches into her backpack and pulls out a handheld radio. "Here," she says. "In case you need help. And here," she says, handing him a pistol.

"I don't know how to use this."

"It's not loaded. And you're not going to have to use it," Fiona says. "I just need you to take it."

"But I can't just shoot somebody."

Fiona turns and moves toward the buildings. A burst of sunlight breaks from the clouds over the cover, flashing brilliantly, like a silver spotlight, into the settlement, its buildings, the side of the ancient cathedral, as they step from the woods.

"Hopefully you won't have to," she says.

Ernie enters
the darkness

Ernie enters the Cathedral Saloon. He stands at the bar, looking up at the rows of exciting and exotic beverages in front of him. What's incredible, he thinks to himself, is how they managed to get all this liquor out here with no road or anything. Do they fly it in? Boat it? Has it been here all along? His eyes settle on a favorite, a whiskey he once took for granted. It has a label with twin seals balancing a circus ball on their noses and smiles on their faces. I've taken you for granted, Ernie thinks to himself, looking at the seals. And now I am back for you.

"What'll you have?" the elderly woman asks from behind the bar. She is cold and unsmiling, her hair tied back in a neat bun.

Ernie stares at the seals on the bottle.

"I'll have a Coke," Ernie says.

"Just a Coke? Nothing in it?"

"No, ma'am. Just a Coke."

Someone rises from a table where two others sit watching, comes up, and straddles the bar next to him, but Ernie fails to take much notice. The Coke comes with a little plastic straw.

"Say, lady friend, another pitcher," the body next to Ernie says, putting an empty pitcher down hard on the counter.

Ernie senses a strange hostile energy, but it doesn't really matter. Now he's absorbed in the array of liquor labels before him—pyramids, mountains, ancient temples. And the colors! Deep browns like reds; clear liquids with just a faint hint of sky blue. It's all enhanced by the smoke, he thinks. I could just stand here and stare at them forever.

"Say, little man. What is that you're frigging drinking there? Is that a Coke?"

"That's right," Ernie says, still not looking.

"Somebody came into my bar and ordered a Coke, little man, I'd frigging shoot him."

"I'll be sure never to visit your bar, big man," Ernie says.

"I'll bet you don't remember who I am, do you," the man says.

Ernie turns and looks. The face is familiar—fat and smirking and trying to pull a beard together. Ernie can't quite place it.

"Sorry, pal," Ernie says.

The man looks across the bar to make sure his friends are watching, then swings the pitcher in an arc. Clearly the fat man wielding it underestimated the speed of the target. Ernie ducks it, and it glances the side of his head, barely cutting his left ear before shattering in a hail of glass and beer on one of the unoccupied tables.

For Ernie, the whole scene quickly spins into motion. The fat man is backed up, he thinks, by the two men he was sitting with when he came in. There is no option but to go past them. Ernie thinks of Eva, of how he's dragged her all the way up here to this horrible, disappointing place, and how he now has to protect her. He has to act quickly, and he does. Three left-handed punches stun the large, bearded face, the third drawing blood from the mouth. As he hits him, Ernie thinks, where have I seen this guy? The nature photographer in Portia? The parking lot at the music fair? Through the swirling smoke, slides quickly flash through Ernie's head. He lunges for his attacker, shoving him back across an old stool and onto the floor. Why is this guy attacking me? Ernie thinks, climbing on top of him and punching him three or four more times in the face before the other two can get to Ernie. I swear I've seen this face before.

Ernie jumps off; the face appears to be hysterical, and he can sense movement around him and feel a tangle of arms and legs reaching out for him. All Ernie needs now is to get to a door, disappear into the darkness, find Eva, explain what happened, and disappear back into the wilderness before anybody finds them, back through the pass, back to Petrolia, to a place with an airport, with connecting flights that send her back to her home, her cult friends, her cult life in the desert, where she's much safer than out here with Ernie. We can just leave her car in the parking lot, Ernie thinks. Maybe he can drive it home for her. Through the smoke and chaos, behind a hurtling bench and table, Ernie sees a door open. I might just make it, he thinks. God damn it, I'm quick! And then something explodes behind Ernie, cutting a neat, hot line between his ribs and his arm. He stumbles, but regains his footing; turning for a moment, he sees his attacker half-lying on the floor, aiming a gun at him.

Just as Ernie gains the door, two bodies enter, but he senses that he is incidental to them. One of the bodies shouts "drop it" in a husky female voice. Ernie runs straight past them, out into the Grizzletown night, and soon the Cathedral Saloon is behind him, and soon, Ernie thinks, as the sharp, stinging pain sinks into his right side, all this Great Gulf Wilderness business will be far behind him.

"Stay out here," Fiona directs Danny from the door when she hears the gunshot. She yells "drop it!" instinctively as she enters the space. All of her training kicks in the second she enters the bar, with one mistake—her eyes, blinded a moment ago by the sunburst and the glare on the beach, take a split second to adjust to the dark interior. Instantly, she inventories her surroundings. There are projectiles—

upturned tables and chairs, beer pitchers and glasses, bottles behind the bar. There are flammables—candles burning along a long bar, a lantern hanging from the ceiling. There are absolutes—a human form she recognizes instantly, on his knees on the floor, waving a pistol in her general direction. And there are variables—shadows of a half-dozen human forms instinctively crouching, looking for cover; and something moving in the shadows to her right, but there is no time for that. At the last second, something instinctively takes Fiona's line of fire away from a dead kill, and she shoots for the subject's shoulder, just above the arm holding the gun. The figure drops the gun, falls backwards, and lies there, looking at his upraised arm. The shadow to her right shifts, and she knows she's made a mistake. And then comes a firm, steady voice from the shadows:

"Drop it, or I'll blow your fucking brains out"

Fiona turns and squints into the darkness. She sees a giant of a man holding a huge wooden staff over his head, as if to swing it down onto her skull, and then gently putting it down on the ground—and behind him stands Danny, totally steady, totally solid, holding the pistol to the back of the man's head.

"Good work, Ranger," is all she can think to say to Danny.

Ernie stops for a moment on the cabin's porch. Eva still hasn't returned, and night is falling. He wonders if she's taken off, found a way out of here on her own. If so, then good for her, Ernie thinks. Maybe she met another bush pilot. Maybe she did find a phone, and David is coming to take her away from all this. It's raining again, a cold, splashing rain. Ernie can hear the dripping forest around the airstrip. The pine trees are black and massive. A last burst of golden light from a distant setting sun breaks through the rain and illuminates the trees, their trunks stained with water. Then

Ernie sees them—Eva's boot prints, crossing the airfield toward the forest road on the far side. She went out to look for him, Ernie thinks. She thinks he went hiking up the forest trail; that's where he said he was going. Ernie takes off as fast as he can after her.

The trail is steep and slippery, the ash still holding onto the rocks and mud. After thirty minutes, Ernie's thighs are burning. The trail has grown narrow from a straight gravel road to a dirt road to a track winding between huge tangles of brush, huge tree branches reaching down from the darkening sky. All the clouds suddenly rip away, exposing a million stars. Ernie notices that Eva's footprints have changed. They are huge and round—bear tracks. She's being followed. He tries to move faster. If I catch up with the bear before I catch up with her, Ernie thinks, maybe I can somehow distract the bear and divert it. And then when I find her, I promise I won't ever even tell her about it. Or if I find her, and she knows the bear was tracking her, and she is unharmed, I will make all this up to her. I will tell her everything. If she will let me, I will ask her to help me.

Ernie races up a hill. At its summit he panics; he cannot see over the top. In the dim star-lit path the tracks continue. At the top of the hill, he looks down. The tracks suddenly stop, veering off into the brush to the right. Eva's smaller boot prints continue, about a hundred yards down an embankment to where he can see her dark form, huddled against the cold, sitting on a rock.

Ernie sits down next to her and puts a hand gently on her shoulder.

"Are you all right?"

"I couldn't find you."

"I know. I sort of went off in the other direction."

"And then I guess I sort of panicked. I just kept walking farther and farther." They look up at the star-lit slope of a perfect bowl of mountains, surrounded by powdered summits. Something flickers in the sky, the first hint of an aurora, or maybe something they both imagine.

"Do you see it?" she asks. "Do you see the lights?"

"Yeah," Ernie says. Everything starts spinning. "Come on," he says, standing and offering her his hand. The pain in the side of his heaving chest is suddenly sharper than ever; he can feel hot blood streaking down his thin ribs. "We'll go back to the cabin. I'll build a big fire."

She takes his hand in her cold fingers and squeezes it fiercely. Then she opens her hand; even in the starlit darkness, she can see blood. "Are you hurt?" she asks.

"I will never leave you here," Ernie says. "I promise."

But as he says it, he slumps back down to the rock, the million stars buzzing like wasps all around him, and he falls into a deep black sleep.

Danny in
the extremities

When he finally sits down, the first thing Danny notices is that the tension that has filled his throat since the events of the previous days is gone. He can swallow again. He can swallow rainwater that drizzles down his head and finds its way between his cracked lips, then slips in cold little lines down to his tongue, then past that thing that hangs there, that everybody calls their tonsil, even though everyone knows it isn't. And because he can swallow now, Danny becomes keenly aware of his immediates, starting with the frost-thin blanket of skin that encases his hot, puffing heart and the warm steel corridors that wrap around his aching bones.

Danny is sitting hunched on a huge slab of granite, jutting out into a dark gulley. The ledge that surrounds him looks like a cupped hand with hundreds of angry thumbs. A swirling, billowing mass of clouds blows up and around and under him, splitting at moments to reveal white phosphorous bubbles. He reaches out to touch it. It's just inches from his hand, but it's really a hundred yards away. The peninsula ends somewhere beyond the last cracked, chipped tooth of the ridge. It's not so far away now. Somewhere beneath this cloud mass, huge waves, rolling thousands of miles up from hot summer seas, are tightening for their big breakup. The waves are about to die, Danny thinks, and they know it, and they will be goddamned if they aren't going to punch something in the face before they expire. Danny can smell them from up here. He can hear them hissing at the rocks. They want to pull this chipped aberration from beneath his feet. They want to drag these black rocks from their violent frozen shelf back to their own sleepy tropics. By then Danny will be long gone, either dead right here or—having crawled back to his little downland life three thousand miles away—dead there.

This, then, is the extremities, the last crumble of land, and I, alone, have made it here. And I am a guy who doesn't exactly see the world in philosophical terms, Danny thinks to himself, looking out at his surroundings. But I sure am starting to get philosophical all of a sudden. Maybe it's this place, he thinks. Maybe it's the cold or the dehydration. Maybe it's the complete absence of humanity.

For a moment Danny remembers the sudden flurry of company experienced in Grizzletown, the gunshots, the outbreak of blunt violence. He remembers how he thought Fiona had blown Chief's head off in the bar, but she hadn't, deliberately. Her shot to the shoulder disabled Chief, and it was enough to make him drop the gun. But she hadn't killed him. Chief, with a bloody nose and a gunshot wound in his shoulder, had lain on the floor meekly while Fiona bandaged his shoulder and called for backup. Afterwards, there was nothing, really, but perfunctory pleasantries from the others in the bar. The rangers let Scout, who had emerged from the shadows, go free; "That's just Scout being Scout," somebody explained. Scout had offered to surrender his walking staff to Danny, but Danny declined. The woman tending bar said she'd never seen Chief before, and the others swore they didn't know him, and they didn't want any trouble.

The bartender let Fiona use a CB radio to call in the seaplane. Two old men in faded army fatigues helped them follow Ernie's tracks through the ash. Ernie and Eva were found together, and while he'd lost some blood, the wound was pretty superficial. Fiona turned to thank the two old men, but they had disappeared. The seaplane came straight into the harbor, questions were asked, paperwork was filled out. Fiona was told by a little bald man with a mustache to place her gun in a sealed bag for evidence; she was apparently in some kind of trouble. Strangely enough, in the bottom of Chief's backpack, crumpled beneath a plastic bag stuffed with every kind of pill imaginable, they found a rolled-up oil painting—it may have been abstract or a landscape or a portrait—but it was sodden and ruined beyond recognition. The painting and a few personal items were placed in one bag, and Chief's gun was placed in a separate bag.

Fiona, Eva, Ernie, and Chief were loaded into the seaplane with two agents and the pilot. The pilot said he'd come back for Danny, but it might take a few days—fishing season down the coast was still in full swing, even this late in August. Danny said he understood, waved them off. Then he turned toward the extremities, the high rocks that remained of the peninsula, jutting straight out into the sea, and he started walking. He walked right past the warning signs. And he just kept on walking.

Now Danny sits here on this ledge, and just three hundred feet away from him, but impossible to reach, in the serrated ledges facing him on the far side of the ravine lies the tangled wreckage of a helicopter. Just a year or two before, it was probably a streamlined orange flying machine, a hawk, a gull darting just above the sea's surface, three or four fragile little people harnessed tightly within its pouch. Their eyes scanned the water's surface and the thin shoreline for other bobbing, dangling, frozen little people, even more fragile, and never more aware of it. The "waffle-asses" Fiona speaks of come out here, drawn farther and farther out onto the peninsula by some strange ideal. They think they're being pulled toward something, Danny thinks, but they're really being pushed away from something. Most of them realize their folly, learn a hard lesson, and head back downland. Some stick it out, and even find a way to live here. But for dozens of waffle-asses each year, the peninsula is the end of the trail, as it is for a dozen or so really brave people who make their living trying to rescue these lost souls and to protect the peninsula from them.

Danny imagines the last thoughts of the stranded. "How the hell did I fall off of this boat or sink it?" "How did I get lost or stranded hiking?" "How did I barely survive the sea or the cliffs or the storms or the ice, only to land here, naked, shattered, my body parts no longer working?" "I need to move on; they'll find me there;" or "I need to stay put; they'll find me here." He tries to picture how this helicopter in its last rescue effort once heaved, winched, sprinted, hovered, buzzed, and groaned through terrible winds, black fogs, blizzards, and the sea. Out here there's no north, south, east, or west. Out here navigation and weather instruments sputter and mumble. Cold breath turns air into vapor, then ice. Water leaps into the sky, sucks rocks from earth, drags trees and boulders and whole islands out into its dark path. For years this helicopter glided safely only with the sea's permission because the cliffs and mountains yielded. For every two people who simply disappeared out here with everything they vainly carried with them, another one was found. Often with their hands and feet frozen into blue blocks of ice and sometimes perfectly still, as if they traveled hundreds of miles from the last strands of civilization just to go to sleep, by themselves, forever.

So now, as Danny sees it, looking at a whole helicopter that suddenly went to sleep forever, he can measure how quickly it must have happened. Caught in an updraft coming up the ravine, one of the blades clipped a rock or a branch, and the whole huge machine side-slammed into the ledges. Nobody inside the helicopter would have had a chance to make so much as a peep. The three-dimensional chopper all but became two-dimensional. It twisted a little, possibly in the short slide it took from its point of impact down the ledge, before nesting on the horns of three or four benign little outcrops and the trunks of a few smashed trees. The impact area was clearly marked. There had been some sort of brief fire or a burst of flame; but very little burns here. The tail was twisted gently above a final tangle of brush, like a human arm draped over the back of a recliner. The bush is already growing around the wreckage, gripping the tangled steel, ripping it apart.

Danny realizes he's been seated here for a while. For three days, he followed the side of the ledges, stumbling along what he thought might have once been a goat path. The ledges terrified him; the farther he went, the more exposed he felt, draped in its sea spray. On a hunch he'd crawled up a shale slide into this rocky little saddle. He glanced down into the ravine, and the fear that he was so far out here, alone, where nobody would ever find him, sunk him down onto the stone ledge. He turned himself around on his hands and knees, determined to scramble back down the ledges, maybe to find the trail again, maybe to find his way down to the beach. And then it registered: Something Danny had been looking at just a moment ago was strangely orange and metallic and spectacular. He'd pictured this so clearly that when he finally saw it, his mind could not verify it. He turned again, and there it was. This could be the helicopter of Fiona's brother—but more likely, Danny realizes, it isn't. There is no reason to report this finding. There are parts of helicopters and seaplanes and shipwrecks strewn across the rocks and beaches of the entire great upland peninsula, from here all the way back to the roads south and east.

For Danny, then, this is the end of the trail, the end of the search, and the end of the peninsula. Danny's had more than enough; he's headed back downland. He's going to have to hitchhike home. Danny tries to picture himself standing in the parking lot of the fish and game building, and Fiona looking up at him, dropping everything, and running, her arms out, tears streaming from her eyes, her golden locks flailing in all directions. He knows this will not possibly be the case.

But as he turns away from the ledges and the wreck and starts climbing back out to the path back to Grizzletown, Danny finds great comfort in thinking that she'll look up from her paperwork someday soon, and he'll pass by in the back of a pickup truck. And Danny will smile and wave, and Fiona will smile and wave back through her office window.

And then Fiona will look back down to her paperwork. She'll shake her head, Danny thinks. "What a downlander," she'll mutter to herself. "What a waffle-ass."

Acknowledgments

In the summer of 1992, I woke up in a tent on the banks of the Chena River in Alaska. I was shockingly hung over, jobless, and homeless. I had gotten there through an increasingly spectacular fifteen-year pattern of bad life decisions. Going to Alaska, however, proved to be the best decision I ever made.

That morning, filled with chronic remorse and black-and-white shadows of the mess I'd left behind, I climbed out of my tent and entered a Technicolor dream world, a mountainous landscape beyond my imagination. Almost spontaneously, I was overwhelmed by the desire to see things more clearly. I quit drinking—forever. I tried to open my heart to kind people and open my mind to smart people. They were everywhere up there—travelers, transients, homesteaders; some there for the summer and some whose families had been there for generations. I was in Alaska for only three months, and I've never been back. But the kindness, openness, and wisdom of the people I met there follow me everywhere. They continue to inspire me to try to be a little smarter, a whole lot nicer, and much more appreciative of every waking, sober moment of clarity.

In my mind, Grizzle envisions an altered history of a very Alaska-like place that might have happened if world events had gone only slightly off track after World War 2. While fictional, the Grizzle Peninsula is clearly inspired by, and infused with, the Alaska that many hundreds of well-intentioned but hapless "downlanders" dreamed of when they set off to find themselves in the wilderness. The northern wilderness is rarely kind to amateurs, and it was even less so in the days before GPS and a quick text message could extricate a fool from any predicament. I'm one of the lucky ones who made it back relatively unsinged. Thank you,

Alaska of 1992, for picking me up, dusting me off, and sending me on my way.

Thank you, also, to the people of Minneapolis-based Flexible Press; to Editor Vicki Adang, and especially to Flexible's founder and editor Bill Burleson. Bill, who is a great author and teller of stories, gave me this amazing opportunity to tell this story. He published my first book, *Shufflers*; and welcomed me into the Flexible Press family—an amazing and diverse group of writers from all walks of life. I'm really proud and excited to be part of this emerging, exciting press. I'm so glad we found each other!

I also want to thank the editors of six journals who published my short stories that were adapted into this longer story-the *Adirondack Review*, *Necessary Fiction*, *34th Parallel*, *Kansas City Voices*, *Johnny America*, and *Cantaraville*.

I want to thank the amazing storytellers of the Moving Pen, a writing workshop I've had the honor to volunteer/lead for the past fifteen years. Thanks to the nonprofit NY Writers Coalition and the Creative Center for Health and Healing at University Settlement (the Creative Center is receiving proceeds from the purchase of this book). I'm so lucky to work professionally with my friends and colleagues at New Settlement in the Bronx. I have benefitted enormously from the support I received from Pen Parentis and the Sustainable Arts Foundation, two organizations supporting writers who are parents.

I am grateful and blessed to live in a tiny apartment in Brooklyn filled with love and laughter and creativity—thank you to my wife Joan and our children Alin, Mariel, and Eirnan. And I am forever inspired and thankful for my first family—my brothers and sisters, Mary Patricia (d), Ernest John, Therese, Anne, Romey, Tom, and Sean—for their perseverance through great adversity, their kindness, and support.

About the author

Downlanders is Frank Haberle's second book; his first novel, *Shufflers*, about minimum wage transients during the Reagan era, is now available from Flexible Press (https://www.flexiblepub.com/shufflers). Over the last twenty years, Frank's short stories have been featured in multiple collections, and they have won awards from Pen Parentis (2011), *Beautiful Loser* magazine (2017), the Sustainable Arts Foundation (2013), and the Rose Warner Prize for Fiction (2021). Frank is a volunteer workshop leader for the nonprofit NY Writers Coalition. He lives in Brooklyn and works in the Bronx. More about Frank's writing can be found on his website, www.frankhaberle.com.